KON TIKKI

KON TIKKI

A SAFE HARBOR NOVEL

MICHÈLE LAFRAMBOISE

 ECHOFICTIONS

Cover design by Echofictions

Cover picture © Michèle Laframboise

Author portrait © Frédéric Gagnon

Inside author picture © Gilles Gagnon

Inside illustrations © Michèle Laframboise

Published by

 ECHOFICTIONS

Mississauga, Ontario

978-1-988339-97-9 Paperback

978-1-988339-96-2 Electronic book

For
Jacques E. Laframboise

my gallant father
who displayed warmth and openness
long before the letters LGBT
entered our social alphabet

1 - GETTING OUT OF THE CLOSET

THE TOOL BARN closet smelled better than Rob had expected, better than the personal hygiene-challenged goons who had shoved him there. The acrid smell of old paint, varnishes, vinegar screamed over the moldy tones of wood scraps, sand and dust. There was also a faint metal tang lingering, that he didn't identify.

Rob's own head was screaming, too, the blood beating at his temples like surf waves invading the beach, then retreating like an hesitant army. A line of pain throbbed on his skull.

He felt his mop of hair, his fingers coming back sticky. He must have laid there for several minutes, if his blood had the time to get solid. A scratch, probably happened when the thugs had pushed him against the gaudy yellow metal shelves he was cleaning off. He hadn't time to register the cut as more blows came down, assorted with stern warnings that *he didn't belong here*!

The thugs couldn't have been employees of the Tool Barn, decked in spotty Tees and frayed, holed-up jeans, a no-no in the confines of a store that catered to a larger public than the hairy lumberjack featured on the sign over the entrance. The store manager had assigned Rob to clear the shelves for the new products, a task that had prolonged his workday into the evening. The other employees had smirked as they left the store, for a "real night", they had joked.

Last week, Rob had refused to submit to a blood test, claiming it was discriminatory. He managed to get a doctor's affidavit that should lay any fear about AIDS or Covid-19 or some unnamed illness to rest. But the store manager had retaliated today, by selecting Rob (among twelve others) for this dreary task.

Working alone, he had assumed the store doors had been locked.

His mistake.

The thugs' must have receded toward the back door leading to the parking. Rob was certain he had checked that door when the last coworker filed out. The back door was a steel slab, impossible to open without a key.

One of the goons must had gotten a key, probably from another employee – no, *associate*, the store manager insisted on calling them. Rob had a fair idea which one most resented his presence, but no solid proof.

He didn't feel very solid right now.

He had curled upon himself after he was pushed down, offering inly his back to the pounding feet. He had not memory of being dragged and locked in this confined space. He had lost his cell in the scuffle, and no way to retrieve it without getting out of the closet.

As he rolled on his side to get up, his belly and crotch sent frantic pain signals to his addled brain. *C.A.!*, he thought, what if those noobs had busted his kidneys? He could die here, alone, of internal bleeding.

Oh, but his sis would have his hide if he croaked! (And wasn't *that* statement proof he was addled?)

≈

Robert "Bobbie" (for his sis), "Rob" (for everyone else) Sundance felt for the cold surface of the closet's door. The faint light seeping under the sill told him the store was closed for the night. As was the whole damn mall.

He grabbed the knob, using the move to prop himself erect. The rustling of his nylon apron, his harsh breathing and the scraping of his shoes on the cement floor echoed loudly in the confined space. He exerted a light pressure on the metal, hoping that the door was not locked.

In the new scheme of design, very small rooms' doors did not have a locking mechanism, so no adventurous child could get trapped inside. Rob knew this was be the case with this closet. The knob turned, a quarter spin, and Rob heard the lock engage. But when he tried to push the door out, the big slab did not budge past a millimeter or two.

Someone had dragged a heavy piece of furniture against the closet door. Probably from the house appliance section.

Rob tried his best to get the door to open, leaning against the surface with all of his one-hundred-forty pounds frame. In vain. That Herculean task would be more suited for his gaming alter-ego. The sweaty barbarian Cog would have make short work of the door with his redoubtable double-headed ax.

But, what Rob didn't possess in brute force, he had in patience. Each of his pushes drove the obstacle one millimeter away.

As he was working, he thought about the uber-handsome blond guy who had come for his paint. That day had been rotten, except for big Stanley, appearing like a sunlight through dark clouds.

Rob had met him at the store, and the tall man was easygoing and amiable, endowed with a wide, generous mouth. Of course, Rob had been smitten by the hunk; the clerk initiated small talk with him, mostly about fishing. The giant had kept it to the amiable level, and Rob got a definite sense of a diverging orientation.

Today, Stan had stopped by with a young short-haired woman walking with crutches. She looked tired, and Rob had offered her to sit for a few minutes, while Stan waited for his paint. She was in her mid-twenties, clearly a stranger, clearly a tourist, and clearly… smitten with Stan, too.

He had overheard her witty discussion with the Christians holding their fetus pics near the clinic next door (the clinic did not do the preg-interruptions they feared, but according to his sis, girls in trouble got there to get referrals.)

The rest of Rob's day had gone downhill from there. His letting a client sit close to the cash register did not stood well with his ramrod straight supervisor from the paint department, nor with the store manager who had been lurking around.

A balding born-again Christian with a Lenin pinch, and scolding eyes, mister Leon wished Rob to get reborn as straight. Rob's supervisor in the paint department was from a similar mix, a military-bearing jock presented as a "true patriot" by the manager. *A true parrot*, Rob had whispered to the kitchenware girls who stood beside him. (Mister Leon was also conscious of assigning proper role models to his flock.)

Not that Rob had ever advertised his orientation when applying for the job. He had combed his unruly hair, shaved and worn a long-sleeve shirt hiding the beautiful ink on his arm.

Inspired by the Wave from an ancient Japanese print, the tattoo looked innocent and artistic at first glance. Only someone peering close would notice the two devastatingly handsome males on the flatboat. *That* had not been in the Japanese print, but Rob estimated it had been a well-invested thousand bucks in New-York city.

He had managed a hair-wide opening. Getting his eye so close his lashes brushed the metal, he could confirm that the big object was a refrigerator box, with a serial number visible. By now, he could work the door back and forth, getting more and more efficient impulse. He could now see the obstacle, a heavy-duty cardboard with an image of the Commodore-Alpha 97 model with twin doors and integrated ice-machine. *You would think it was a spaceship instead of a fancy refrigerator.*

He kept on bearing on the door.

The opening had reached about three inches when the refrigerator stopped moving. Rob pressed his shoulder and groaned, but the Commodore-Alpha 97 had returned to Immovable Object status. He racked his brains to understand what was blocking the fridge box. He was tall enough to see over the top of the box if he stood on his toes.

The distance between the box and the nearest rack should have been wide enough. So he guessed the thugs had wedged another product behind the box.

He sighed. Again, he rose on his toes to peer over the box's edge. The closet was located at the back of the store, next to the employees' break room. It opened into an alley that faced the front window.

Rob could see a portion of the mall through it.

The Tool Barn lights were closed, but there were lights in the mall. He could make out the bright avocado-green and pizza-red and banana-yellow and orange-juice ensigns of the fast-food outlets at the other end of the big interior plaza, a lost space. Most were open, but the apparel and clothing stores were shut down. If he channeled his inner Cog, he could still get off the closet, then back to the change room to ditch his uniform, and off the store before the mall itself closed.

He snaked his arm through the opening, and waved it up and down. Maybe a security guard would see him and get him out. He would have a master key for such emergencies.

He could not see much higher because the fridge box limited his line of sight, but a few changes in the light told him people were moving around, sampling the goods (urg) of the fast food joints. There were always a handful of plastic bag-laden strollers taking their time looking at the displays, a fact that gave him hope.

Rob pushed his arm farther, feeling the angles bunch his sleeve and bite into his shoulder. He tried to wave in a wide angle, but the edges of the door limited his moves.

"Heeey! Heeeey! I'm stuck!" he shouted at the top of his lungs.

After a time, he staggered back, his head swimming in a haze. He could have a concussion. His foot struck the hairy brooms waiting there, their bristle brushing against his calf, and the rubbery cords of recently used mops.

2 - FISHING AROUND

JOSH TALLGATE, descendant of a proud line of Maori warriors, had not often set foot in the mall, except for some pressing needs and bits and pieces of hardware. The owner of the Kon Tikki Bar and Restaurant had to do many errands himself to keep the place afloat in food and booze.

Certainly he had never eaten at the row of fast-food outlets counters, like the Thai with its wasteful boxes of sticky ramen, that a clutch of teenagers seemed to enjoy. He crossed the emptiness of the central plaza, a wide bowl of air four stories high. The distant ceiling bristled with metallic light fixtures like threatening porcupine spines. Among those spines, hidden loudspeakers dripped a sappy Musak tune that diverged far from the original *Cry Me a River* original.

The opening day at his restaurant had been a whirl wind of visitors and officials and cooking, and their food reserve had dwindled to almost nothing in mere hours. Josh had come at the new mall to find a food provider closer to his restaurant.

Josh stepped with his empty bags inside the Safe Harbor Fresh Food Mart, next to the Divine Authentic Thai Experience. A moody ballad from a pop singer echoed in the mid-sized store. From where Josh stood, near the open sliding glass door, the moody ballad clashed horribly with the sappy Musak falling from the plaza's hedgehog ceiling.

The fishes on display at the sea food counter were indifferent to the ugly mix; a spotted bass stared at his shaved head with glazed eyes, as if they had seen too much. The other fishes on the bed of plastic grass looked oversized to him, injected with growth hormones or what-ever the fish farms used to get them twice the size of their species in the wild. In reverse, the "captured in the wild" salmon was smaller than the specimens his old restaurant had served. Maybe there were less of them left, with all the net-dragging methods of fishing that scraped the floor.

Josh bent over the counter, breathing in the fish smell, with a tinge of salt. He looked for signs of deterioration linked to storage, like dun scales, or fibrous branchia. The glass-eyed fishes glistened as if some oil had been applied on the scales.

The clerk from the Safe Harbor Fresh Food, his complexion also oily, looked at his thick leather watch. He was probably not used to a customer spending more than four seconds poring over the goods.

"So, you takin' some fish or not? I'm closing soon," he said.

A pale-skinned clerk, no more than sixteen if Josh a good judge of ages, was pushing the fruit and veggies stalls across the sliding door threshold.

Josh turned his attention to the glassy-eyed bass, the pale undersized salmon. He would have to drive soon next

8

morning to the next town, maybe even try the fish markets of Portland to find the kind of fish he wanted. Even in a tourist district, he wanted the best for his clients.

He shook his head and turned away from the counter.

"Thanks, but no thanks," he said.

His grandfather, still living in the New Zealand, had developed an intimacy with the sea and its creatures, instilling in the small Joshua a love and reverence for the great ocean. And a sure taste for the cooking of seafood. When his dad had migrated to the new World, the boy had been disappointed by the lack of natural, accessible coasts. He had been more disappointed with the lack of fresh fishes. Those in displays didn't taste real.

He would need more fish since the grand opening affluence had drained his reserves. As he was exiting the grocery, his sensitive ears caught a stray snippet of conversation over the background music.

"Did we show that fag, or didn't we, hey boys?"

The talker was a teenager in frayed jeans who had tried to achieve a Crocodile Dundee look and failed. The leather vest was just too slick-looking despite the grease stains. His hair was a half-inch fuzz covering his skull that suggested a GI Joe attempt. He and his similarly inspired buddies were destroying boxes of ramen at the *Divine Authentic Thai Experience*, laughing and chattering between themselves, sharing some private joke.

But it was one word, *fag*, that made the hair on his arms bristle.

Josh had left New York city, where the Pride parade was a genuine festival and only some pockets of resistance had not gotten the rainbow-colored memo.

Here, in this town closer to the ocean, he felt he had become an exception, again. But the seated boys were not looking at him, engrossed in their food and smacking their lips. They looked like idle lazy bums who would splash dark paint over beautiful murals, just for the sake of defiling it.

Josh listened in, nevertheless.

It had been a survival reflex at school in the Island, before his dad swept him and his mom to the States. It had been a survival reflex as well in the bad neighborhood where they lived, as his dad work inhuman hours while waiting for his green card, and his mom cleaned two-story houses in the affluent district (always under the fear of being sent back to the Island). Then the word fag faded out from the public discourse, as the LBGT letters rose to prominence, later followed by the Q+, at the same time his parents achieved their own dream. Josh's dad never ceased to remind him how lucky he was to be naturalized.

Josh had graduated from the Culinary Institute with honors, worked ungodly hours in restaurants, before opening his own place in the Big Apple. It had been the best days of his life, inviting his aging pair of parents to his big opening...

A burst of raucous laughter erupted from the tiny table, so loud that the brown-uniformed security guard eating at the Coffee Place two fast-food joints from the Thai rose from his counter stool and started ambling in their direction.

The fuzz-haired youngster with the Crocodile Dundee vest saw the old man in uniform coming their way and whispered to his buddies.

The three youngsters rose from their plastic chairs and swaggered across the plaza towards the doors, leaving flattened boxes behind, some ramen wriggling out like tiny worms in the hot sauce dripping from the upended containers. The tension drained from Josh, but he followed the trio with wary eyes.

He had witnessed the same close-cropped style in counter-demonstrations where born-again fanatics allied with worthless thugs tried to disrupt the Pride Parade. He had seen such closed-cropped head bunched in front of a coffee place or restaurant popular in the gay crowd.

Josh started to pick his own way around the stools and lost packages to get out, leaving a distance between him and the young men. Passing under one harsh spotlight from the bristled ceiling, they looked older than ide teenagers. Their pale skin colored golden by the yellow sign with the hefty, confident-looking worker on it. The Tool Barn would be closed by now; however, the idle youngsters elbowing themselves and sniggering, their heads swiveling to look inside. *Maybe casting the place for something to steal,* Josh thought.

Then the trio passed beyond the double doors of the mall into the night, leaving their mystery behind. Josh inched closer to the great front windows on his way to the double doors. He slowed down to an easy amble, wondering what could have been so interesting inside the store. The big overhead halogen lamps had been shut down; only the light from the plaza's weird ceiling entered the store.

There was enough of it to make out the chest-high shelves with small tools hanging on tringles, the paint station, some boxes of mid-sized appliances, all straight alleys leading to the back…

From the corner of his eyes, he caught a movement.

Josh froze, one foot lifted. There big sliding door of the Tool Barn was closed. He checked the big horloge over the double glass doors: the Barn had closed more than thirty minutes ago. Nobody should be there.

Putting his bags down, he leaned against the glass, peering inside. Then he saw it.

The hair on his arms and nape bristled, like a mini ceiling. Over the appliances boxes, a head with lanky gray hair was hovering, seven or eight feet up.

In an instant, Josh remembered all the ghosts stories his grand dad had told him. A shiver ran through his spine, that had nothing to do with the abusive air conditioning of the place. His heart stammered, in readiness to run from a danger.

The head was moving, jerking this and that way, the horrid hair strands trailing along. Josh could see no face, only the hair in the gloomy light. Moving, swaying, along the dripping musak. He could make out a slim neck swaying along, the body hidden by two coffin-sized cardboard boxes. He felt sweat forming over his scalp.

Almost crashing his nose against the glass, Josh observed the rotation of the head. It was jerking, up and down, the move constrained by a narrow opening over the coffin-sized box.

He wondered if the headless youngsters had seen the ghost, too. If the head made them laugh.

As soon as this question had formed in his head, his rational self came bravely forward. The trio had not seen a ghost. As his eyes accustomed to the penumbra, the hair strands became a mop head, the neck a handle. The jerkiness had a weird human touch in it.

A terrified, helpless human.

3 - CALLING OUT

I<small>T WAS</small> a damn shame that the very visible and orange bristle pad of the floor brush was too wide to pass through the opening. Rob had managed to wedge one of the worn mops through, the dank water trapped in the strands resisting his efforts with a squishy noise, sending droplets on his hair.

The young man's arms were shaking badly, his muscles tetanized by the effort of waving the mop's handle over his head. He couldn't see if someone had seen his signals, because of the visual obstruction, and there were no ladder inside the closet to grant him a higher point of view.

Rob wished he could have pushed back the door a tiny half-inch more, enough to ease his forearms out of the closet. His moves would be less constrained then.

But he couldn't stop to pause because, soon, there would be no one left in the mall; even the security guy would lock the place and retire to his office on the third floor.

So Rob gritted his teeth and carried on, cursing under his shortened breath. For a time, pure anger filled him with a Hulk-like energy, and he saw himself as a powerful warrior, unbreakable, the image of the tall barbarian drawn on his arm.

Then, his sugar levels dropped as did the anger, and Rob's moves became sluggish. He was breathing hard, his lungs filled with the musty closet air, his arms trembling like a Parkinson sufferer's. His sweaty palms glided on the handle. He let it drop down, the squishy strands stuck against the box edge.

Maybe it was useless. He considered dropping down and making himself comfortable for the night. He could not even call the store manager to apprise him of the situation.

Not that the manager would have cared that much about *his kind*. Rob had made sure to wear long sleeves after the comment, so no one could see the wicked drawing on his left arm. He took solace in thinking of the design, the big wave with foam and droplets, and the boat, with the two men hugging each other, obviously to ward of the storm slanting their craft. He had loved the original print. Looking down at it took him far away from the realities. It had been worth the pain from the needles and ink, the long wait between seances.

Since he had dropped out of law school, Rob shared a flat with his sister, who worked at the diner place on Ocean View. She would get worried of he didn't come in at ten.

Thinking of his sister, of the anguish his absence would cause her, made him pause. He grabbed the handle and resumed his exercise (in futility, it seemed), hanging his hope on the plaza's still-open lights. His eyes burnt, as some droplets from the mop head landed on him.

What if there were no one left? He couldn't know for sure, his sister would tell him.

He was breathing so hard that he almost didn't heard the new sound. A muted *bang* coming from the from the store-wide vitrine.

Then a series of *bang, bang, bang!* echoed, the sound of a palm tapping against the thick pane of glass. Someone was banging against the glass with enough strength to transmit the muffled sounds inside the dim-lit store.

Hope, relief flooded Rob's heart. He pursued his valiant efforts with the mop, waving the tufted head higher. Then something else washed over, a familiar spell of dizziness. His blood sugar levels were acting up. His morning insulin shot must have been spent in the exertions. He had *no more spoons left*, as his mother would say. And his insulin pen was out of reach, stuffed in his backroom locker.

Like a weary child, he had let go of the mop's handle, not even wondering why the mop didn't fall, and curled on himself.

As his visions clouded, his last conscious thought was that someone was actually *caring*.

4 - CLOSET ELF

Hey, what are you doing?

Josh froze at the querulous tone, his meaty fists stopped mid-distance from the vitrine. He could see the moist imprints on the glass, evaporating. He turned, in a slow motion, keeping his hands in view, palms up.

Like he had learned to do when walking or driving alone in trendy New-York neighborhoods, all brimming with white cops who couldn't recognize the chef of a celebrated Luck Traveler. When Rafe was with him, however, the same cops would treat them like visiting royalty. But then, Rafe's Testarossa or Kia would attract envious gazes.

The guard's uniform fabric had a dark Demerara sugar tone that clashed with his pasty skin. He wore no beret or cap, but his balding dome shone under the porcupine-spine fixtures of the mall's center. The corners of his mouth were downturned in a sour expression.

Josh looked about the brown-sugar uniform for a firearm, but the guard carried only a short stick. He felt a marginal relief, as he discarded the idea of being summarily shot for loitering. He had become aware his chocolate skin upped the probabilities of meeting with a fate similar to the teenager shot by a white man while crossing a property.

He chose the direct answer.

"There's someone inside the store," he said, gesturing toward the interior.

The officer ambled around and, keeping a wary eye on Josh, cast a quick glance in. The mop had stopped moving.

"I don't see a thing," the guard said.

Josh couldn't shake the feeling someone was there, and hurting. Maybe even unconscious, the way the mop stopped moving.

"There's someone in the closet. Probably wounded. Maybe you could check?" Josh said, in his most amiable voice.

The guard squinted.

"Yeah, sure, I should unlock the door to let a bum in?"

Josh had had enough. He picked up his bags, full of fresh vegetables and vibrant salads.

"I am Josh Tallgate, owner and manager of the Kon Tikki," he said.

The restaurant's opening had been promoted by and large, so the name struck the guard. He licked his gums.

"That the new place on the pier? My bro told me the food's great."

Josh nodded, and saw an opening.

"Yes, and I would never let one employee locked in," he said, keeping an eye on the mop strands. "What if they found a corpse tomorrow because you didn't act?"

The threat of the responsibility, of negligence, prodded the guard to a conciliatory attitude. He looked up Josh again, noting the black apron with the lobster logo, and the name in red letters printed over it. Finally he looked away, having decided the tall brown man was not a threat.

"I guess it can't hurt to make a short check. But you stay out."

Josh nodded. He stood rooted as the guard used his row of small cards to tap the door mechanism. Whatever happened to the good old metal keys? Finally a clack sounded, and the paunchy man stole inside, clicking open his lamp. Josh followed as his bald dome floated over the shelves in the alleys, then stopped.

He heard an expletive. Then the guard retreated and got out.

"Mr. Tallgate, there's definitively someone breathing in the closet. But there's a heavy box blocking the door."

Josh followed the smaller man in. He stood next to the mop head wedged in the crack of a door, the strands splayed over the carboard of a fridge box. The box was not alone: a mid-sized box was stuck between the larger, coffin-sized box and the base of a shelf support. The screwed-in base prevented anyone from pushing off the boxes and free the door.

He looked around, to locate any hand truck, flatbed pushcart or even forklift that would move the coffin-box. There should be one such tool in a store this size, but he didn't find any.

"Can't move the damn thing," the guard said. "But, with your help…"

Josh rose on his heels to peer at the crack, over the top of the fridge box. The inside of the closet was dark, the bulb probably out. But he could hear a low, rasping breath.

"Hey, hang on in there," he called out, trying to imbue his guttural voice with reassurance. "We're getting you out."

It took some work to dislodge the smaller box, its sides announcing "the freezer of the future". Josh recognized the make with the double F imitating an old Fantastic Four logo. It contained a smaller storage unit, but still quite heavy. The fiftyish guard was perspiring as they pushed it out of the way.

"Those frikkin' fridges are so damn heavy," the man huffed, as he looked at the coffin-sized box.

Josh took a look at the perspiring guard, a textbook example of a candidate for an acv.

"Let me do it," he said.

The security guard wiped his brow.

"Thanks," he said. "I'm not twenty-five anymore."

Josh braced himself against the side of the box. He groaned aloud as he pressed on, his body forming a perfect 45 degrees angle against the vertical surface, the imprint of his fingers sinking in the dun cardboard.

He pushed, and pushed with all his might, his legs banded. The box was incredibly heavy. Josh felt grateful for his gym sessions and the constant exercise running a restaurant required of him: lifting boxes of cans, hauling bags of potatoes, pushing tables and chairs around, hooking the fluo nets in place.

He was pouring sweat when the friction resistance gave in, and the fridge moved, inch by inch, the base of the box emitting a papery groan.

Josh thought that it would have taken two or three men to pull it in place. Especially as the appliance section was at the other end of the store.

At last, with a triumphal *Han!* the hefty obstacle had cleared a space wide enough of a man to step in the closet. The store lit up at the same time: the guard had found the master switch for the store.

The halogen-white overhead lights fell the jumble of cleaning tools in the storage closet, the shelves full of toxic detergents, the round soaking pail, the fallen mop, over a prone, unmoving body facing the wall, one arm draped over his torso, the hand invisible. A smell of acid cleaning fluids, urine and turpentine pervaded the space.

Was he too late?

He had heard horror stories of guys dying in confined spaces, where fermenting grains pulled all oxygen from the air. *Do not put yourself in danger*, his reasonable part told him in his father's voice.

Josh held bis own breath, long enough to hear the soft breeze of the air wheezing from the man's lungs. A young man, he saw now with the lights on, clad in a sweaty Tee-shirt and apron of the store with the Tool Barn logo. A mane of flame hair was all he could see of the head. He took a sniff at the air, but beside the turpentine, coming from a badly closed can, he did not identify any poison.

As a cook in training, then as a restaurant manager, Josh had had a first responder formation. He bent over the clerk, to check for a head or neck wound. He touched a strand of hair sticky with blood, that he retraced to a scratch at the back of the skull. There was no artery hemorrhage, as the blood had caked.

He squeezed one shoulder, feeling the bone under the thin fabric.

"Hey, hey, are you there?"

No response. The store clerk was still unconscious. Josh delicately turned the young man into a recovery position, one hand cupping the head while the other pulled the shoulder.

Doing so, Josh felt a jolt of surprise.

The slender arm attached to the shoulder wore an

artistic drawing of a wave, the white foam done so elaborately that he was reminded of the Island's sea, and his gramp's fishing boat. The ink covered one forearm, the wave rolling up the elbow to swell around the biceps in a "sleeve" tattoo pattern. The light was strong enough to let his eyes roam along the blue-green wave, the flat boat, the two men aboard, clinging to each other for dear life as the wave rushed over their heads.

As the young man's face came in view, Josh felt a more familiar jolt, one he had felt a few times in the big City.

The store clerk's face had the surreal purity of an anime character, or an elf from those Tolkien tales, ivory-skin with a smattering of pale freckles under a mop of red curls. Josh had almost the urge to drag his finger along the pale, unlined skin, from temple to the tip of the triangular chin. Wide-set eyes rested under long lashes, also glowing the same soft orange as the brows. The pale budding rose lips were thin, but well-defined, half-opened over pristine, regular teeth.

Josh almost expected those eyes to spring open, showing enormous, watery dark pupils over blue or green itises. He was not aware of the wild thrumming of his heart, until the guard's voice startled him.

"Is he OK? Should I call an ambulance?"

Josh almost jumped out of his skin, his hand slipping from the shoulder to ram on the floor. He tamed his beating heart before answering.

"Yes, I think we should—"

"*NO!*"

The power of the single syllable shook both rescuers, even as Josh felt the reed-like body getting taut under his arms. Presently, he turned to the voice, and

and

21

couldn't
tear his eyes off.

The closet elf had the most unusual eyes Josh had ever seen, better than an anime character's, the irises a liquid, icy blue that was the exact complement of his fiery hair. For a second, Josh sensed a powerful will at odds with the reedy frame of the young man. The blue eyes tore through Josh like lasers, scanning him over like a shelf produce.

And Josh suddenly hoped those uncanny, icy anime eyes liked what they beheld.

Then the brows drew up, and the incredible power seeped away, leaving only naked fear. Josh felt the same change echoing in his own body.

Shit, he thought.

5 - DREAM WARRIOR

IT WASN'T the first time Rob's diabetes acted up; his morning insulin shot was a distant memory for his too-active body. Staying late and getting assaulted hadn't helped restore his strength. He was dehydrated.

As he lay curled against the wall in his weakened state, a familiar darkness invaded his mind, a confusion of exhaustion and despair clogging his thoughts. As his head kept pounding, red and carmine swirls danced under his closed lids, with flashes of grinning faces.

Lame, they had said.

Faggot, maggot, others before them had taunted.

It has been a nightmare, ugly and violent.

Hey! Hang on in there.

A voice was calling out. Distant, but powerful, carrying a tiny kernel of care embedded.

Like the banging, before the darkness engulfed him. He was stuck in a rowing boat on a heaving sea, about to capsize. Maybe he had dreamt the voice.

He felt himself sliding in and out of consciousness.

Steps, and grunts. One raspy voice, cursing: *frikkin' fridges, so damn heavy!*

Then the rough voice, calm, resolute: *let me do it.*

Rob liked this dream. It definitely beat dying alone in a closet.

The irony of the situation almost made his dream-self smile. He had grown up in Safe Harbor, discovered his orientation abroad while studying law. Various shenanigans ensued, until fellow straight-As students had outed Rob, leading to him getting expelled by a clutch of morally-tight, tenure-track-academics from another century. Despite his straight-As results.

Fast-forward to a five months stint in New-York as a seedy underground bar server, long enough to get his wear-able artwork and get roughed up in a few bar brawls. And then back to case one, in a small town where secrets were hard to keep.

Where someone else had found out about him. And angry hands had found him, too.

Hands on him.

Right now.

Hey, hey, are you there?

A shiver ran through his curled spine.

Not rude hands. A gentle touch.

The universe dipped and swelled as someone moved his head and shoulders. A massive someone, biceps ballooning against his back. The skin exuded a faint smell of sea and fish. He thought about the blond fisherman, discarded it, because a fisherman rising before the sun would be home at bed.

Then he felt safe enough to unclench his eyes and peer under the veil of his lashes. A ruse he had used countless times at school, seemingly asleep, eyes wary, ears pricked for danger.

Oh, brother!

He was safely enclosed in the arms of a powerful Edgar Rice Burroughs-type warrior, one huge arm supporting his throbbing head. A pair of grave brown eyes were fastened on his own, giving off an equal mix of fascination and concern.

The man's features looked like a perfect sculpture etched in brown mahogany wood, the cheekbones leading to a strong chin. He was bald, the curve of his cranium emphasized by two fierce spiked tails rearing up over the ears to curl at his temples. He gulped. That dream warrior was a dead ringer, no, a *very alive* ringer for actor Jason Momoa but without the dreadlocks, with a hint of Dwayne Johnson in the smoldering eyes. One tiny silver ring protruded from his left eyebrow.

Casting a discreet look down the arms, Rob noticed that the snakes were actually dragons, stylized, long empty contours entwined around both arms, each scale drawn in loving detail that must have been painful to drive in the skin. The background of the dragon was an intricate swirl of roses and knives and fishes and other motives he couldn't identify. He thought for a moment: a Asian gang member?

But all that paled under the gaze roaming over him, a gaze both warm and compassionate, at odds with the harsh features and fierce tattoos.

Then another voice broke the charm.

"Is he OK? Should I call an ambulance?"

An alarm bell rang in his brain, as a flux of adrenaline chased the weakness away.

Leaving the mall in an ambulance would be the end of

him. Emergency transport would eat the last of his savings. Rob had no personal insurance, and the Tool Barn franchise had a shitty health coverage for its "associates" that barely covered his insulin. If he lost the job, he would have to pay his insulin shots.

All those thoughts zoomed across his mind as the big warrior-like man holding him turned to answer.

"Yes, I think…"

Rob's whole body tensed from the adrenaline influx. He shouted a ear-shattering *NO!* at the two men looking down at him.

The man in a security outfit, old Doug who couldn't run after a thief if his life depended on it, recoiled. The Conan-sized warrior shivered as if struck by thunder. The thick fingers tensed on Rob's shoulder, as his dark brown gaze plunged directly into the young man's eyes.

His examination took the same time as Rob's own.

Rob passed his tongue over his teeth, to give his sugar-fogged brain time to compile what he saw. The tattooing artist who worked on the big arms had taken advantage of the extra surface available there. He had had lots of time on his hands to produce such intricate, Yakuza-style patterns. C.A.! Rob was envious.

The dragon's sinuous bodies bulged over the soccer-ball-sized biceps, the spiked tails running up his nape and over the ears, almost meeting at the brow. The rest of his head was free of ink, the crown cooked by the sun to a darker tone. Scattered dark hair lingered at the edge of the temples, a hint that the tattoo had been etched around the stranger's hairline. A mane that, for some reason, the man had shaved.

Shaved heads were still all the rage, but Rob sensed this warrior had not cut his hair to conform to fashion. Considering the horrid heat that plagued Safe Harbor for weeks, and it was not even the heat of summer yet, practicality must have won.

All those thoughts shot through his brain in mere seconds, just as old Doug's hand was reaching for his cell phone.

"Please don't call!" he blurted, his throat still raspy from his exertion.

6 - MR. HERCULES

PLEASE DON'T CALL, the young redhead said, his voice taking on a frantic schoolboy's tone. "I need this work."

"But you bumped your head," Josh said. "You might be injured."

The young man passed one hand over his tousled hair.

"No, I'll be OK. It's nothing, just a spell. Need to get my pen."

"Huh?" Josh said, puzzled.

"My insulin pen," he said. "In the back room."

The clerk struggled to rise, folding his slim legs. Josh pulled him up and helped him walk out of the stuffy closet. Doing so, he noticed the button with the cheesy *HI! My name is ROB*.

"You must be thirsty, er, Rob" Josh said.

The young clerk nodded, as he leant one elbow on the smaller appliance box.

Josh bent over the back pack he had tossed aside before tackling the fridge box. He pulled a water bottle (refillable) and proffered it.

"I didn't touch it yet. Go on."

The clerk —Rob— tipped his head backward. Josh watched his Adam apple bobbing up and down as he emptied the liter, his incredible eyes closed in pure relish. Then, he gave back the empty container, his fingers unexpectedly brushing against Josh's hand.

"Man, you *were* thirsty," Josh said to cover the trouble he felt at the hand-to-hand contact.

"Almost like he spent three days in the Sonora desert," the security guy said.

The elderly man's face was as weathered as Josh's grandpa's had been.

"The tap water here tastes bad," the young man said. "Too much sulphur."

Josh had noticed the odd taste of the local drink water, but for now, he was noticing too much of Rob. The angle of the jutting collar bone, the way his russet curls moved, the bluish veins drawing a map of rivers on his neck that Josh's lips itched to follow…

"And how did you end up in that closet?" the guard asked.

A thin smile lit up the young man's face.

"Hey, hi Douglas."

"What happened?"

Rob made a raspberry, which gave him such a childlike expression that Josh found it hard not to smile. Then the closet elf shrugged, crossing his arms over his chest. Josh noticed that only one arm bore a tattoo.

"Nothing, just another wonderful day at the Tool Barn," the young man said, parroting the jingle of the TV commercials.

The guard's weathered face got more weathered.

"Were you, er, assaulted?" Douglas asked.

"Mister Douglas, I just had a dizzy spell in the closet. "

The agent smirked, his head inclined.

"Yeah, and then those two heavy fridges just up and planted themselves in front of the door!"

Rob stretched his thin lips in a too-wide smile. At this point, he looked to Josh like a mischievous, carrot-haired Tom Sawyer.

"You're a cool dude, Mister Doug, but I *do* need the income. If I were to blab about getting jumped on and locked in, without witnesses, the boss would have my hide."

The older man's brow got wrinkled, puzzled by the answer.

"But…"

"It's OK Mister Doug. Just don't report it."

The slender elf's voice had returned to its calm.

Josh recalled how the three pals had looked and pointed in the direction of the store. But he hadn't actually *seen* them beat Rob, and neither could he force the victim of a hate crime --because that's what it had been-- to come forward.

His blood boiled in anger, his fingers crushing the straps of his backpack. He would have stomped those three goons, if he had known. The red freckled boy's face, and reedy frame compelled a strong protective urge inside Josh. But at the same time, the icy, mocking eyes held him at bay, like a force field or a Star Wars Jedi mind trick.

The desert-weathered faced guard sighed. Maybe he had had children who did not heed his advice.

"I won't tell a soul, Rob, but I still have to close the mall at nine."

The elderly guard shuffled out of the store, his shoulders slumped. Josh felt by osmose the powerlessness that many older men felt regarding the younger generation.

Rob hefted himself over the lower box.

"Mr. Hercules, can you get my insulin pen?"

As he tried to come with a witty answer the red head fished into a pants pocket. He proffered a tiny scrap of paper.

"This is the combi of the third locker from the left."

Josh scanned the numbers.

"Huh, ain't it dangerous to leave those on you? Anyone can open your locker."

Again, came the impish smile that managed to both shock and excite Josh.

"You're right. Subtract two from each."

Josh did not have to explore the place long before finding the row of employee lockers, near the infamous sink. Nor did he need to count from the left: Rob's locker was covered with fresh graffitis, *fag* and more unsavory words sprayed with black and red paint. The thugs had targeted him.

He passed his finger: the damn paint had already dried.

Even the combination lock had been sprayed, but Josh could see the numbers and managed to unlock it after two tries. The inside was clean, and he found a thin wallet and a thick stylus, like an orange vaping cig. He hurried back to the redhead with the two objects.

Rob took the stylus from him, his slim fingers brushing against Josh's.

He punched some part of the apparatus. Without hesitation, he stabbed himself in the right thigh, through the pant's fabric. His face did not move a muscle. Josh shivered at the idea of pricking himself every day like this.

"Thanks, Mr Hercules," the young man said, pocketing the wallet.

Josh harrumphed.

"I'd prefer Josh," he said. "Josh Tallgate," he added.

The impish elf took his proffered hand. His grip was more energic than Josh had expected.

"Well, happy to meet you, Mister Tallgate, and your dragons, too," he said, his twinkling eyes scanning the intertwined water dragons tattoos covering his arms and rising to the back and sides of his head. "Real cool design. This your Chinese sign?"

"Huh," Josh said, still dazed by the young elf's audacity. "Is that stuff acting fast?"

The young man slid off the box, and stood erect. The crown of his orange hair was level to Josh's breast bone. For a moment, Josh itched to grab those shoulders and press that head against his chest.

"I'm OK, now," Rob said.

"Well, I guess I'll be on my way, then," Josh said, in a fake conversational tone.

Except his legs would not follow his words. He had to pry himself from this impish Tom Sawyer-elf.

"And, thank you again, for getting me out," the elf said.

Josh finally succeeded in lifting his knees and moving his legs forward, toward the sliding doors. As the young clerk close the glass door behind him, showing no weakness, Josh turned.

"Try to stay out of trouble," he said.

Again, the cheeky smile lit up, just before the snap of the door and the tick of the locking mechanism.

Bravo, what a lame rejoinder! Josh thought somberly.

Rafe had been the one good with words.

As he crossed the wide plaza, a lamenting song dripped from the spiny ceiling. He felt as if he was walking away from the warmth of a small sun, heading into the cold, unforgiving outer space.

7 - DATING SCENE

When you were a small guy on the dating scene, you had few choices: you either compensated a short stature with a rascal attitude, acting tougher than nails, spouting swear words like candies.

Or you slinked around the popular handsome hunks, hoping for an opening line that would seem unthreatening.

Rob touched his sweaty hair. The gash would be difficult to explain to his sister, but the metal shelving unit in the closet could act as a fair alibi. Mel was too protective of him anyway, as if *she* was the older sibling instead of her baby sister.

He had not found his cell, and had come to the conclusion that the thugs had decided to pad their accounts with some quick money. Tomorrow, he would check the Easy-Peasy Money Mart outlets for his stolen cell. Not that here would be a ton of those in small Safe Harbor.

He started on the two kilometers that separated the mall parking from the second-story flat Melinda and him shared in the "boondocks" of Safe Harbor. In the dark of the summer night, it was a long walk. And the foul lighting the mayor had added to all the public spaces hid the stars.

Nevertheless, Rob felt like smiling.

Man, was that Tallgate hunk worth every scratch he got! A real dreamboat, like the ones he chased at parties, arts openings (with food) and the bars, some time ago.

When you're small, sometimes getting into a fight with bigger men attracted the right, chivalrous kind of hunk. He really relished the sensation of manipulating his bearded *baras* rescuers into thinking they found him.

Of course, Rob never actually picked a fight with a stranger.

He just sat at the counter and nursed his drink until an argument between two patrons got heated (and in an election year, it was a sure bet, and *heated* was a lame word for the exchange). He then managed to get in the immediate proximity of the flailing fists, kind of like entering the orbit of two colliding stars.

Inevitably, one fist or two connected.

That was Rob's signal to wade in, distributing his own goods, expecting to receive more blows than he gave. He had learned to protect his mouth first, because he didn't care for a dentist's hefty bill more than any other. However, he often wound up with a split lip or bleeding nose. The best would be a cut over the brow, that bled like a hose to cover half of his face.

And always, after the brawl subsided, a kind stranger would pick him up and ask if he was OK, and similar questions, and if Rob played his cards well, he would get a warm bed and company for one night. Or more.

All brawls did not have such a Disney-an ending.

More often, the kind stranger would call (and pay!) a cab for poor Rob, and he wound up alone in his own sky-high rented cubicle. Another tumultuous time, Rob had crashed a high-end party at a posh hotel in honor of those Splendid Siblings the artsy-fartsy scene was raving about. He had spotted a cool silver fox type, but he got spotted by some shady, overbearing producer before addressing the hunk.

Glasses were broken, bottles crashing down, a brawl ensued.

Rob remembered going down in the fight, along with the cool silver-haired guy he had an eye on, with more muscular dreamboats stepping in.

But the silver mane had ended up talking and schmoozing with a dreadlocked hunk that Josh would not have minded going out with. Nevertheless, the silver-haired guy had slipped a green note in Rob's hand for a cab.

He had looked in stupor, having expected Jackson's long pale face, and finding a jovial Franklin on the hundred dollar note.

Not all defeats were absolute.

Rob walked, his tummy still throbbing from one well-placed foot strike. He could hear some night club music wafting from open doors, the heat granting permissions to pollute the calm streets with rowdy songs.

Getting assaulted by strangers -- and Rob counted himself fortunate his thugs had been the kind of religious nuts that got their sex drive urges taken care of elsewhere – had not been a pleasant experience. He had protected his face, but the metal shelf had left its imprint on his brow. He would have to wash it in the closet bathroom he shared with Mel's hundreds of perfume bottles and cold cream pots, all marked "specimen". From the time when his sis worked at a pharmacy that sold more skin care than cough syrup.

As fate would have it, Mel was hunkered in a 1920-s style chesterfield reading a mag, her brow only marked by two vertical lines. Worried about him, but not too worried as in call-in-the-cops way. She had showered and changed from the diner uniform where she worked in daytime. Her low-heeled pumps were waiting by the door.

He tried to slip in, his gait as natural as usual, but his attempt at discretion failed when his foot struck a discarded magazine. The cover featured a Godfather-style guy with sunglasses, sandwiched between similar Mafioso-styled suits. The three sported wide grins. *The murder still unsolved*, the caption said in blood-red letters. *A waste*, Rob thought, because that dude had been handsome. With a winning smile like that, why did he have to coddle to mobsters?

"Hey bro, did you find a bar worthy of your time here?" She asked, knowing full well the response.

Safe Harbor, butt-end of civilization and intellectual light, had only three bars, none of them catering to his kind of crowd.

He was still thinking about the bald bara type and his soccer-ball bicep when he became aware of Mel talking.

"Huh, what where you saying?"

Mel's keen brown eyes measured him from head to toes.

"My, but you were in a brawl, brother! Tell me all about it!"

Her tone rode in a precarious balance between, *oh-cool, you reverted to your old ploys* false cheerfulness, and a more savage *Robert Sundance, when will you grow up*?

Rob nodded to the two meanings.

"I'll talk after I wash," he said, then scuttled off to the tiny bathroom.

Once inside, he leaned over the sink, its borders over-populated with tubs of toothpaste and skin creams, some of those he would need, even if their best before date was expired. Mel had explained there was a security factor added. But then, for non-edible products, nothing changed much, except the texture.

Then he looked a the mirror and sucked in air.

He hoped Mel had not noticed the fiery red spots on his cheeks. Then, he fished out a face towel and ran the hot water on it, thinking about what story he would tell her.

8 - MEDITATION ON THE PIER

Liar, liar, liar! said the gulls.

Josh completed for himself: *pants on fire!*

Early Saturday morning on the pier, the place was deserted except for the gulls who, somehow, thought the contents of the canvas bags Josh was carrying contained their own breakfast.

His steps echoed on the graying wood boards. The calm sea had not yet gotten the memo to rise and shine, despite the low clouds passing from a deep slumbering purple to the dark red of a cauldron left unattended on the stove.

He passed the Kon Tikki entrance, two steps then the enclosed terrace, noting the damn birds had left whitish, gluey offerings on the tabletops.

He had though it great to have an open-sky place, to forget about the stuffy VIP room of the Lucky Traveler. Rafe's buddies often congregated there in the late evenings, talking quietly under a cloud of cigarette smoke (ignoring the non smoking signs). Each time Josh had come to explain the menu, he had felt their eyes trained on him, in a way that made his skin crawl with goosebumps. But the sole danger came from a guy always coming up with ways to diss Josh's cooking. Despite him being hailed as one of the best chefs in the city.

Now he understood why the other shops and eateries had elected to keep an actual roof over their client's heads.

His previous experience had been in the busy city of New York, where the flying rats kept watch over the back-yard dumpsters. Along with the four-legged rats and raccoons, too.

He hadn't seen any rats or raccoons yet, but the damn gulls more than compensated for the absence of rodents.

Josh lifted the heavy link chain closing the terrace entrance (more a psychological barrier than a real one) and passed the L-shaped bar counter, protected from bird dropping by a corrugated roof that extended from the previous restaurant's kitchen. He congratulated himself for not tearing down that metal roof over the bar and stools, and keeping the kitchen at the back as it was.

He unlocked the thick wooden door and pulled it open, leaving the saloon-style flap doors in place. The gleaming metallic freezer and fridge looked like twins. He distributed the contents of the bags, only vegetables, to the storage place.

The opening had gone well with the mayor attending. Maybe too well. Josh had made a bundle and had to get to the bank twice, but at eight o'clock they had run out of cods, crabs and salmons. And lobsters, as Henry the cook had boiled the last one.

After his empty foray at the mall, Josh had found a grocery open late and stocked up there at ungodly prices, storing the goods at this place for the night. It had been a chancy decision to close the Kon Tikki that early on a

Saturday evening, but he couldn't feed his clients thin air and potatoes. No more than he could leave the bar operation to his rookie cook, Henry. Josh had learned the subtle art of mixing drinks from the best.

At his other place, he had left someone else do the errands. And do the accounting. Here, he had started from scratch, and decided this time he would see to all. His seed money was his own, and he checked the numbers twice, even if accounting was not his forte. Josh had been only to happy to leave that chore to his associate…

Liar, liar, liar!

Josh exploded from the kitchen.

"Shut up!"

He waved a dishcloth in a wide arc to scatted away the stupid gulls perched on the tables. The flying rats flapped their false-angle wings and left, not before gracing the tables with fresh spoors.

Josh wondered about adding roasted gutted gulls to the menu.

He stopped by the bar the check the cupboards under the counter. The cash register was locked (and empty), as were the display of liquors. Rows of glasses hung upside down, well-scrubbed; the sun rays hitting them would reveal any neglected spots. The Kon Tikki did not even try to cater to the morning crowd: it opened at eleven and closed at ten, seven days a week.

Working 7/7 was a necessity, as he had to train Henry to his ways, and the waiter hired for the grand opening had left.

Josh creaked his lower back and took advantage of the early hour to explore the pier.

The long finger of civilization extended well into the water. His place was the third from the end, next to a trendy coffee shop outlet with sky-rocketing prices, and the pastel front of the ice-cream counter. The service window was closed, but the forecast of another hot day would spell good earnings for the couple who operated the place. Either Vera or Anton Dorowski would stand at the window.

The end of the pier looked over the marina, an orderly quay that almost paralleled the concrete breaker extending like a protective arm against the wilder waves of the ocean. He could not see on the other side of the breakers, only the lonely light tower at the end.

He had expected to find one or two oldsters fishing in the quietness of the morning. His grandfather had passed all his mornings on his small quay, wary of the birds angling for his catches. Little Joshua had loved going with him, waving his stubby arms to keep to hungry birds at bay.

At this time, the gulls only said *Caw, caw, caw.*

The benches, carved with a good number of hearts and initials, would be a perfect place to sit.

But no one was fishing.

Most of the boats moored were the leisure yachts or sailboats, their sails furled. Amidst their pristine white hulls, a few colored crafts stood out. Extravagant fishing boats, or older models. Josh spotted one empty berth. Someone was out at sea, fishing. Or trying very hard to.

The gentle, rhythmic *sloosh* of the waves crashing against the pier's posts lulled him away from the worries of launching a new restaurant. He could retreat to a blissful time, walking on the hot sands with his grandfather.

He had wanted to make a new start in a remote fishing town, far away from his previous location in the hubbub of New-York. And of his associate…

His late associate, that is.

Josh's nails, cut close to the skin so he would not get dirt or food scraps under it as he tended bars, dug into the weathered wood of the railing.

It's only for the job, Rafe had said. *Just this once.*

Oh, how Josh would have loved to have a time machine, hurry five years back and yell *don't go!*

Rafe had been the brain of their outfit. Raphael had the good looks of a star, with premature gray hair that crowned his handsome face and twinkling gray eyes, kind of a younger Michael Douglas.

After years of secretive teen crushes, and repression, Josh had blossomed in the free atmosphere of the big Apple. He had roamed the gay scene, tried all the bars where his size drew attention.

But hot young guys were hot young guys; Josh had met Rafe at the losing side of a vicious brawl that had erupted at a too-well attended art launch, set in a grandiose loft.

Some bums had crashed the party, drawn by the free booze; the promoter had called security to get them out; mayhem and spilled drinks ensued. An assistant barman for the catering, Josh had been manning the buffet. A tall gentleman had plunged in help a small guy getting clobbered by security men and other excitable attendees. The silver haired man had got his suit ripped in the process, collecting some nasty punches.

Advantaged by his sheer mass, Josh had waded in in his cook uniform, his white bonnet flying off, to rescue the gentleman who was bleeding profusely from the nose. As the brawl subsided, he admired the way the older man gently helped up the small guy and sent him on his way. Josh had picked up a bunch of napkins from the buffet table, and proffered them to the heroic gentleman. As he was dabbing at the blood, a pair of incredibly pale eyes (the red and violet lights hiding their true color) had locked on his own… and that was it for Josh Tallgate.

Raphael Giordani had been a dozen years older, but as much in love with good food and fine drinks. And also in love with good sex, Josh had been surprised to discover. Rafe spoke in a quiet but confident tone of voice that felt like honey dolloped on his skin. Even without the good looks, Rafe's teasing voice was enough to send him in a tumult of desire.

The idea of starting their new hot restaurant blossomed a week after the brawl. They drew plans. Rafe, who worked in real estate, made a round of enquiries about places to let, and visited banks for a loan. In no time at all, the silver-maned man came up with a place in an impossible location, and the seed money for the start up. They had feasted that night on mussels and caviar, and the very rare bottle of Valpolicello.

Josh had not asked how Rafe had qualified do fast for a loan. He had assumed that, as a real-estate agent, Rafe knew the channels to borrow money. If only he had known where that pot of gold had come from…

Liar, liar, liar!

The damn gulls were at it, circling over his head, waiting for an offering.

Maybe Josh *had* had a whispering intuition about an irregular arrangement, but he never asked. He had been too busy with finding a trendy name, hiring employees, an assistant cook, checking the food sources…

Liar, liar, liar!

And, he must admit it, too head-over-heels in love with Rafe.

For two wonderful years, life had been as perfect as it could be for Joshua Tallgate.

His parents were elated when their son invited them over to taste his fine foods, installed at the best table, in a secluded room overlooking the river and the lights of the city. His dad had already known about his orientation, and he approved of the handsome silver fox Josh had befriended. Rafe had a way with words and could charm his way out of a snake pit, and to a mother's entrenched heart.

After so much misery in their life, his tired parents were ripe for a piece of happiness, and Josh would be eternally grateful to Rafe for providing it.

Josh and Rafe were the cream of the New-York trendy restauration scene. Invited at every art show. Josh's well-combed dread locks had graced the cover of *American Food* and *Kitchen Trails*…

Until the fire.

Liar, liar, liar!

Josh pumped a huge fist toward the birds, who were not impressed at all. For a second, he wished he had a gun, like Rafe did. His friend had a carry-concealed, for safety reasons, the same reason why he also hid his same-sex relationship from his traditional family.

That had only added to the younger Josh's excitement at the time…

The sun was still hidden under the horizon line, but a fan of rays extended high, announcing the main attraction, the lingering clouds glowing a red and orange.

Orange, like the fire against the dark of the powerless neighboring houses, the silhouettes of the fire trucks. Police cars lining the street. The TV crews, like vultures on a scent of death. Watching from his hotel room two states remote, Josh had prayed no one was trapped inside the inferno…

No more of that. This is the past.

Josh leaned over the railing.

A yellow-brown blob caught his attention. He remembered the middle-aged woman ranting about the waters being too nutrient-rich, devoid of fishes. Josh hadn't understood how "nutrients" could be bad for the fishes, but he had listened with the patience cultivated by his years of bar tending.

The gray-haired woman, gaunt and as tall as any normal guy, had shown him pics of the supporting structure under the pier, and of species of medusas drifting south. That had gotten his attention, because his father, and grandfather, warned little Joshua about toxic jellyfishes lingering in shallow waters like tiny blue goblets filled with poison.

The yellow, waxy blob bobbed out of his view, under the deck, destined to strand itself on the unforgiving beach. That kind of medusa he didn't know well, but he had seen similar ones on boards lining some Maine beaches.

Then, the morning called itself to Josh's attention, as the whole sky lightened to a warm orange, lighting up a host of puffy, golden-lined clouds that looked like celestial freckles.

Since yesterday, the orange-haired anime-faced boy had dwelled in his thoughts. That pointed, elfish face under the rusty reddish curls, the slender grace of his arms, those lashes, as red, like the rest of his body hair, lent to other, more luscious imaginations.

Josh chased away the thoughts. The redhead was probably underage, working a summer job to pay his school fee.

Liar, liar, liar!

A flock of gulls passed over, one of them holding a conspicuous silvery fish in its beak. Then, he noticed it wasn't a flock: the other birds, all adults, their plumage white as white, were diving and pecking at the one with the fish. Josh winced to get a better view: that one was had brown marks of the chest and wings, and caramel-colored head. Probably a first-winter bird. Young, and talented, but the more experienced adults had banded against him to get his catch.

The younger one defended himself (Josh had no way to tell the sexes, but he had instantly felt a connection to this bird) but eventually the whiter adults prevailed, and the "brownie" flapped away, doing its best to ignore the triumphant calls, as the rest dispute the choice bits.

White robed nuns and priests, they called me brownie, his granddad had said.

The brawlers at the bar had called Josh *nigger*.

Josh Tallgate steered his gaze to the sea, to the white-capped waves rushing in, where the lone gull etched a neat silhouette against the orange-tinged waves.

I may be a liar, but you're just a bunch of thieves.

9 - LAST DAY

ROB SUNDANCE GOT out of home clean as a new penny, after showering and washing his hair. Checking his reflection in the oval mirror, he had the satisfaction of looking his usual merry self. No trace of the attack showed, and his hair hid the cut.

As he walked the distance to the mall, he reflected upon yesterday evening's events. The last night had been filled with dreams featuring the handsome stranger. He didn't know a thing about him, except his name.

To be honest, Josh Tallgate could have been hetero. However, the way he had returned Rob's gaze, helping him out of the closet, had tilted Rob's inner compass. The sheer contrast between this huge, steeled body and the delicate care Josh had shown, still sent shivers up Rob's spine. He had asked the man to fetch his insulin pen, enjoying his company a bit longer.

He had also enjoyed the stunned look on Josh's face when he had punched the insulin pen against his upper leg. Rob was used to it, but Oh boy did that stab make an impression on the warrior-built guy! He wondered if Josh was a tourist, bound for another place. Tourists tended to be open about his orientation, at least, more open than most locals who hadn't gotten the memo yet.

The man had had the looks of a regular gym user. Alas, there was no gym in the mall, not yet. He crossed the wide, wasted empty plaza, checking out the missing stores. The basics were here, sure, one Pharma, one clinic besieged by the fanatic army, one grocery, two trendy cloth outlets, and the Tool Barn.

The store was already opened, and Rob let himself in.

Rob got the first inkling of a reversal when he found the two large appliance boxes, awkwardly posted near the closet. In the haze of the aftermath, getting his insulin fix had prevailed over the rest. C.A.! He *should* have asked the big guy to stay, and push back the large Commodore-Alpha 97 box to the right place. Even if Rob had remembered to put the fridge in its right place before leaving, there was no way he could move the things by himself.

But there was no one there, except the store manager, and his office door was close. Maybe he could take one of the dollies and get the bigger fridge back. Rob rounded the box, and zipped to the back room.

That's when he discovered the state of his locker's door. C.A.! This would be a cinch to wash out, if he could lay his hands on the right solvent. He averted his eyes from the scribbled insults as he opened. He put his wallet and new pen in, and locked it back.

As he walked to the storage with the dollies, he heard his name called out.

Leon had come out of his lair, sniffing an easy prey. His flabby arm shot in the direction of the closet door, obstructed by the fridge boxes.

"Mister Sundance, what are *those* doing here?" he said, flexing his syllables like vocal muscles.

Rob racked his brains for a creative answer.

"Well," he said, "I thought I saw a rat back there, and wanted to make sure there were no more."

He made sure not to talk to fast, or too glib.

Leon scratched his Lenin goatee with his index.

"Really? As if you didn't know the proper procedure in case of rodent infestation?"

Rob swallowed his pride. Yes, there was a protocol to follow in case of a sighting, and he should have taken the store phone to call the manager. Because an inspector visit could prove fatal for the business.

"I, I forgot," he said.

"Then there's the defacing of your locker, this night."

"But I didn't do it!"

Too late, the young man understood the trap. The store manager squinted, appraising him as if he were a strange color.

"Then, if not you, who did it? I left you in charge of this store, for a reason."

Yeah, so I would be alone in the store and get jumped, Rob thought.

"Because, despite the rumors, I trusted you as a responsible young man."

Rob was stymied by the load of crap spouting from this man's pie-hole. Leon had never, e-ver trusted him. The Tool Barn outlet manager had found out about Rob's rainbow-colored orientation a full three months after he had hired the young man.

Too late to slack him after a "training" period. The young clerk couldn't be certain about Leon hiring the thugs; that would be closer to Rob's snarky coworkers in the paint department, and closest to military-ass Rudy's style.

"Alas," the manager's voice purred, "it seemed I made a mistake with you."

His mellifluous voice told Rob he had found a pretext. It was not the first time, and Rob had managed to hang on the other times. Even his refusal to take AIDs tests had not stuck, with the help of the friendly doctor.

"Sir," he said, putting steel in his voice. "I completed all the tasks you gave me. The hand tool shelves are in order."

Leon's fingers stroked his goatee in an almost obscene fashion.

"You lied about the rats," he said. "I'm certain of it. Besides, the floors are clean."

Rob pinched his lips close. He *could* admit he was not strong enough to push the heavy boxes all the way from the appliance section. He could admit evil doers had entered the premises. Lots of good such an admission would do.

"Yeah, boss, look what I found," another voice chimed in.

Rob would have loved to have Josh or the old Doug with him to witness. Rudy was the epitome of what the young queers everywhere feared, a rough haughty virtuous veteran, so far gone to the edge of the political map he had fallen over the edge. In his fifties, he boasted about two tours of duties in 'Ghanistan and Irak.

Rudy had entered by the parking back door, his gum shoes soundless, the best to surprise a lazy employee, er, associate.

The virtuous veteran in the light, and that's when Rob

recognized with a start the small white bag, he was holding in his paw. Where the heck did he find *that*?

The store manager's eyes bugged out. He grabbed the bag, and took out a flat pink box of contraceptive pills.

"This is outrageous," he said. "Where did you find those sinful objects?"

Yeah, Rob thought, *of course it is sinful to limit women's reproductive freedom.*

"Why, under the employee's coffee machine."

C.A.!, thought Rob. The heavy coffee machine was a choice hiding spot. Eliza should have taken the thin box as soon as she found it. Did someone spy on her?

Rob had gotten the contraceptives to prevent her from getting pregnant by her boyfriend, a boyfriend who didn't take *no* for answer, but poor Eliza was hopeless in love with the curd. And her trad-values family was adamant about maidenly virtue.

For Rob, getting her the pills had been damage control, pure and simple.

"Sin, pure and simple!"

The manager cast the flat box into a waste bin. It landed over a pile of paper towels without a sound.

"You know we can't condone any sexual relation inside this store," mister Leon said. "The girls of the kitchenware and bathroom department are young, naïve things, easily preyed upon by a cute boy."

Rob let an innocent smile stretch his lips.

"But, by now, you also know I'm not swinging that way."

It was the first time Rob had alluded to his orientation. He heard a chuckle behind him. The presence of the Douche, a sour-looking guy from the appliance department who sniffed coke in the hangar. And loved to see another take the flak.

"But your kind is known for spreading ill conduct!" Mister Leon said.

Rob refrained from rolling his eyes.

Sodom and Gomorrah all the way again, he thought.

Dragging footsteps told him that another associate had joined the fray near the two large boxes. Steve from the small tools department, with an stench of mice and tobacco. Rob wondered if he still had lice in his oily black hair. In the his eyes, the same gleeful spark shone. Steve had been the one supposed to stay afterhours yesterday.

A sinking feeling clutched at Rob's throat. This time, he might not get of the hook. He made a last-ditch effort to defend himself.

"I don't know about this box, sir," he said.

The Douche chuckled again. Steve displayed his bad teeth in a smile, sharing a private joke as dirty as he was.

"Really?" the big Rudy asked, his hands wrinkling the angel-wing white pharma bag.

The virtuous veteran ripped it open, pulling up a thin slip of paper.

Rob felt the blood drain from his face. He remembered how yesterday morning, Eliza had taken ill. That was why she didn't take the package. And Rob had been distracted, in a hurry, and forgot to take the receipt from the little pharma bag. Of course, the evening events had made him forget the white bag.

So much for being a white knight, he thought.

Another chuckle from the Douche echoed.

"And, lo and behold! The receipt is still attached, paid by a Robert Sundance."

"So now, it's a federal offence to buy things?" Rob said, crossing his thin arms over his chest.

He knew he was done for, even if a judicial dispute could conclude to the discrimination. But a legal battle would eat months and years of his life, and not worth the sour atmosphere of this workplace.

He felt really sorry for nice Eliza, who would not get her month's ration of pills.

Mister Leon was talking. Or rather, preaching from an invisible pulpit.

"…We can't allow this conduct in our store."

Then, he conclude his speech in one Trump-style bellow.

"You're *fired!*"

A pregnant silence ensued, like the one preceding a round of applause. His shattered it.

"This is just a pretext," he said.

"You'll get your pink sheet in the mail."

The manager showed him the front door in a flourish. The mall was not open yet, so no clients would be around.

Instead, Rob stood as straight as the veteran, and walked towards the back room.

"Hey!" the Douche and the store manager protested.

"I have the right to take my things, and my insulin," Rob said. "Unless you want to add thief and endangering my life to your obvious discrimination."

He went to the back room, opened his smeared locker, took wallet and pen. When he came out, the Douche and Steve were rolling away the Commander 1997 to its rightful place in the home appliances department. Mister Leon had retired in his lair, and Rudy's voice was swearing at some supplier in the truck bay, his voice echoing.

Nobody was looking at him. As he passed the waste

bin, Rob retrieved the package, his task made easy by the bunch of paper and towels padding the bottom of the container.

He shuffled out, weaving in and out of the alleys, until he spotted the straight brown hair of Eliza, with an armload of powder blue baby towels. As he approached, her heart-shaped face took a questioning expression.

Rob shrugged, and made the cutting sign across his throat. Her lips shaped a soundless *Oh*, her hands clutching the towels to her bosom. She knew her life would get more "complicated" (her ubiquitous word) without protection. Rob put a finger on his lips.

He glanced around, before slipping the tiny package in the deep front pocket of her uniform's apron, his move hidden by the pile of towels the young girl was holding.

10 - BEACH JOB

THE SAME DAY

Rob was walking about the beach, casting some stale chips to the hungry gulls, after a filling meal at the place where her sister worked. At the door, he had encountered the same close-cropped girl with the crutches, she having finished. She had had recognized him and asked about his job, and looked so empathic that he almost blurted the truth to her.

The diner had a cool Mom and Pops atmosphere, and the couple owning the place treated Mel as a daughter. He wondered if poor Eliza would not be faring better here. At least, she would have his proud sister hovering nearby.

He had taken the morning to update his resume, then had walked out in widening circles to check out some quick-cash places similar to Easy-Peasy Money Marts (that Safe Harbor did not have one of those was a mixed blessing). His cell remained unfound. The problem was, he didn't want to work at the mall anymore, so he felt sorry for the shy angel. He had tried his luck at the diner, but they were full. However, Mel had suggested they take advantage of the fair weather after she finishes her shift, at two.

So he was waiting for his sister, walking the length of the beach where a gray-haired woman un faded jeans and tee-shirt was picking up small items from the sand.

Rob kept looking for the big warrior-like guy who had shown him compassion this morning, but no bald head or dragon tattoos over muscled arms were visible among the tourists.

He didn't care for the afternoon beach crowd, the jocks and the inflatable dolls in too-tight swimsuits. He had spotted such a couple lying about, too pale to be locals. And too young: the boy fit and ripped in a natural way that would never come back if he let himself go to waste, even with protein shakes and gym sessions and coaches. His blond girlfriend's navel had not yet sunk under the tiniest layer of belly fat.

Maybe they were students: he spotted a thick book near the girl's hand, without a garish cover of a popular novel. Her opened bag showed more of the thick kind. The ripped boy was hunched over a similar manual. Not undergrad students, those, to study in summer.

"Ogling the tourists, bro?" a joyous voice piped in.

Mel had not changed from her uniform, but retired her nameplate. Rob was quick to free her from the two lattice folding chairs she was holding. They found their favorite spot, near an exposed part of the Old Man's face, a scarred expanse of smoothed rock, as far from the parking lot that they could.

The tide was reeling in more refuse, plastic and dead fishes, and dead things that the gray-haired lady was picking up and putting in the bins on the child's chariot behind her.

"So, bro, tell me all about it."

He had not talked much in the diner, not wanting to have his sister worrying while balancing all those plates on her arms. He had imparted the minimal info, like he had to the nice girl with the crutches.

"There's nothing much to say, sis."

Lame-City, here I come, he thought.

But Mel had a way of seeing through him as if he were made of glass. She half turned on her chair, the sand squished between her toes, to look at him through her pink sunglasses.

Melody and Robert Sundance were almost twins: they had same pointed elfin chin and blue eyes, and the red-orange hair both got from their Irish-ascendancy mother. Except Rob sported more freckles than his younger sister. Melody had always been the savvy one, and she had accepted Rob's orientation way more easily than the mother had.

"C'mon bro. What happened to make you leave a job you've held for a whopping eight months?"

What she didn't add was that it had been the longest position he had ever held. Even his server stint in N.Y. hadn't been that long.

He pondered his answer. He absolutely did not want to brooch the subject of the attack.

"Someone found out about me."

Mel's right heel stabbed the sand.

"And that's no ground for dismissing someone."

"In some States, if there are religious concerns, it is. My working there hurts the preset beliefs."

"In other words, you boss is a noob," Mel said, fingering absent-mindedly the small roses-encrusted crux that was her favorite (because no dead or dying guy on it).

Mel's words surprised Rob. His sister had always had a religious trait in her, but less zealous and with a wider worldview than most Christians. And she would not allow any guy to rule her like shy Eliza did.

"Not only the boss," he said.

"Who outed you?

Rob did not answer. He gazed at the empty sea, at the lazy circles of the birds, white gulls and darker cormorants. He heard Mel sigh.

"I told you to hide your ink, bro."

There was nothing worth replying after that, so Rob stretched his legs and leaned back, looking at the sky, contemplating if he had a future in Safe Harbor.

His half-closed eyes fell on three persons huddling by the chariot, close to the rising tide.

The gaunt woman in the faded jeans was hunched over, her rounded back turned to him, her shoulders shaking.

Crying. In public.

Rob could feel her humiliation like a mud layer solidifying over her form. Her jeans was covered with moist sand, her hair covering her face.

The blond girl he had noticed earlier was close, one slim hand on the woman's shoulder. She had pulled a short and Tee over her skimpy suit.

"So sad," Mel said. "I come here for my breaks and there she is, picking up the jellyfishes and the scraps. Alone."

Rob squinted to follow the action. The jock had joined the women, changed too. He wore one bright yellow tee over his long trunks, lugging a red ice box. He plunk the box down and fished out a water bottle from it. He gave it to the woman, who drank greedily.

Case closed, Rob thought. But it was nice to see some compassion at work.

A whimper of pain came to him, carried by the wind.

"Shit," Mel said. "Sore back. No way she can finish today."

She got up and folded her chair. Rob felt tired from the day, but he summoned his will to follow his sister. They picked their way through families and frisbee-tossing youths. When they got in range, the gray-haired woman was talking about gloves. When she bent over the bins, she winced, one hand pressed on the small of her back.

"You'll concentrate on the plastic, and I will pick up the jellyfish."

The girl shook her blond curls.

"You just sit tight," she said. "Tell us what to do."

Of course, there was nowhere to sit comfortably for her. Rob unfolded his chair and plunked it in front of the woman. He remembered seeing her before, but had never talked to her.

"Here's mine," he said, grinning under his mop of red hair. "I'll help, too."

The woman had a strong face lined with worry, and the dray in her short hair was uneven. But she turned radiant eyes at Rob. She pointed to the box.

"Gloves first," she said

Mel stepped in.

"Got some for me, too?" she asked.

IT HAD BECOME KIND OF like those happenings on YouTube. Once four or five persons joined, others drifted by, mostly teens, and one family with two ten-year-old. Soon, a small crowd was at work.

The woman, Kathleen, distributed gloves and instructions from her chair, like a queen. She took special care to tell the parents to keep an eye on the children and away from the shore. And no bare foot, please!

Some teens present had were recording and broadcasting with their phones.

The sturdy hospital gloves Rob wore did not hinder his finer coordination as he picked up small items like colored bottle caps, bits of broken glass, spent elastics, plastic bottles, used condoms (sigh), all going to the garbage bag he was trailing.

As he stretched himself to rest his back from picking up litter, Rob noticed people against the railing of the pier. He was close enough to see the sun glinting from the phones and cams they were holding. Oh, the joys of Internet!

The Safe Harbor public beach extended two full kilometers, the sand looping around the tongue of rocks. After the initial shove, the family and some teens had peeled out, leaving their half-empty bags with the seated woman, Kathleen. Mel was talking with her. Rob took a new garbage bag and headed to the far side of the beach. As he rounded the sloping rock slab, he noticed campers stretching palms-covered towels over the smoother areas of Old Man's rock. The high tide would soon lap the rock, separating the far end of the beach.

His path crossed the cool ripped guy in sunglasses, Alan (Rob had to learn all those new names).

"Take care," he said as he passed Rob on the thinner and thinning band of sand. "There's two Lion's manes and one blue bottle jellyfish that need to get in the big can."

The young man's bag was full to burst. Rob nodded,

reminding himself that this handsome jock was already matched, and plodded on.

He found the two yellow blobs laying like deadly sunbathers on the moist area. Waves licked his running shoes as he wrestled the things inside the bag, their floppy gelatinous mass making for an awkward harvesting. Especially as Queen Kathleen had warned them in a stern voice about the mortal danger the floppy masses presented.

He smiled. Almost like his mom. Rob missed her. She wasn't dead, but his dad had never accepted Rob after the "college shenanigans" happened. He had cut Rob out of inheritance, out of every thing, and warned him to stay out of family gatherings. Out of a warped sense of loyalty, his mother had stayed aloof, only sending a Christmas and birthday cards.

Out of a resolute sense of loyalty, Melody had left the house, wounding up here while Rob was gallivanting in New-York. Gallivanting was Mel's gentle word for his actions. His father had another one, but his mom never let a dirty word cross her lips, or stain the paper of her letters to Mel. (She would at occasion slip one envelope for Rob in those letters.)

Rob had landed at his sister's flat after one needless brawl had landed him in the hospital with a broken ulna (not, to his relief, from the tattooed arm). After he was released, he found his tattoo parlor closed, the owner arrested on some tax charge. Rob didn't need his other arm done anyway. Like a tired animal, he came to winter in quaint Safe Harbor.

11 - A CLEAN SLATE

JOSH WAS WASHING his hands for the nth time, before tackling the cutting of the pricy cod he got from the distant grocery. Too many distractions around him, too many worries circling over his bald head like vultures.

A clean slate, he had said to himself, over and over.

He had emptied his personal account to get away, and changed his appearance. No one from Rafe's "family" in N.Y. should be able to retrace him here. The old restaurant had been set up in Rafe's name: at first, he had felt hurt that Rafe had not signed him as co-owner. But the money was flowing in, the clients happy, the critics raving: that was all that counted.

After the fire, he had figured out that Rafe had tried to protect him from retaliation by the unsavory crowd he hung around.

Nevertheless, Josh had the reflex to check any passerby that seemed to be loitering, kind of like a woman fearful of an revengeful ex. There may have been one such loiterer in the crowd at the opening, but the mayor's presence should have dispelled any doubt about the legit status of the Kon Tikki.

That's when Henry had come from his restroom break, excited, his fly not zipped up yet.

"Seems like the Boy Scouts are there in force to clean that beach," he said, mopping his wide brow with a hand towel.

Josh had been working to get up to date; lacking one man, he had met and seated the first clients. Now he wanted to make the fish palatable, not to the clients, but to facilitate Henry's work. He had forgotten to put his Help wanted sign. The chef would appreciate some assistance, too. Henry had not finished getting acquainted with the Thermidor PRG486 48-inches gas stove that Josh had bought to replace the Precambrian oven the old *Mama's Sea Food* had used.

They were only two men, and Josh had to mind the cash register at the bar counter.

The rumor of excited voices finally got the better of him, and curiosity won.

"Can you check the place for a minute or two?" he asked.

Henry was cutting a head of salad his ribbons, moving so fast his hands blended.

"Sure thing, boss."

Josh hooked his apron at a crochet under the bar counter, checked that the cash register was locked and the key in his jean pocket (not in his apron). Then he crossed the small dining terrace, descended the three steps separating terrace from promenade, and went for the railing to se for himself what the ruckus was.

Scores of swimsuit-clad tourists were combing the

sand, plastic bags in hand. A portable boomer spouted rhythmic measure of Gypsies.

Youngsters, mostly, seem to fan around an gray haired woman seated like a boss, giving orders, instructions. With a shock, josh recognized the gray-haired, hard-faced woman that had bickered with the mayor at the grand opening. Her visit had proved instructive, to say the least.

A young red-head in a short green dress was bent over the woman, talking with animation. Josh did not hear a word, except for one teen who whooped "Free pizza!" and typed furiously on his phone screen. That's when Josh's exerted eyes identified the neat short-sleeved top with the white collar, the sturdy nylon of the skirt: a restauration uniform.

Thinking about his own needs, Josh swung back in the Kon Tikki, knotting his black apron in place. He switched jobs in the kitchen, helping Henry prepare the plates for the couple on site. The portions were ready, and Josh carried the steamy plates on the terrace.

"Here, Mr. and Mrs. Porter, your fish and chips, and your sole," he said. "Enjoy!"

The lady, who looked a few years south of ninety, had folded a fabric towel on her lap.

"Thank you, young man," she said, offering a kind smile. "My husband loves the fish, and also cheesecake. You don't serve desserts here?"

"Not yet," he said. "But someone told me the Safe Harbor Hotel serves to-die-for cheesecake. If you go in the afternoon, there should not be a crowd."

"A judicious advice," the husband said, nodding his balding head, his hands closed on the handles of fork and knife like weapons."

Josh ducked back in the kitchen, instructed Henry to keep an eye on the nice couple, and help them negotiate the steps in case of need. He had not thought about accessibility when searching for a suitable location.

Now, if he was very lucky, he would find an able server.

12 - HELP WANTED

THE REDHEAD WAITRESS LIFTED her fresh face as Josh approached. The seated woman looked up in alarm.

No wonder. Josh should have taken a bag or something to grab, because he didn't exactly know what to do with his hands when he was not holding a shaker, or a kitchen knife or pan.

So he took care not to walk too fast, keep his hands in his pockets, and avoid the boombox-carrying kid walking around. In his stretched jeans and black tee, with the dragon tattoos reaching to his bald head, he looked like a thug, the kind that a Tarantino movie hero would make short work of, just to show off. The kind who in the streets of New-York would scare a frail old lady...

No that old, Josh corrected himself, as the gray-haired woman rose from her chair.

When he reached her, he had a shock. She was on the gaunt side, but almost as tall as he was, standing in her faded jeans. He gaze was a light shade of blue mixed with gray, with a net of sad wrinkles about them. She had taken a step forward, one hand supporting her lower back, a gesture Josh had seen hundreds of times in restaurants. Sore back.

"Are you coming to help, too?" she asked, her wary expression adding "or cause trouble?"

Josh raised his palms in a placating gesture.

"Er, yes, I would help, but it's…"

His eloquence stopped there. His gaze had fallen on the young green-robed waitress, and caught on a familiar haunting shade of orange. Some red-haired people had brown or black brows, indicative of a mixed parents or coloring lotion. But this one was a true redhead, her eyebrows barely marked with crayon. And he had seen such a undisputed red hair no later than this morning…

He felt both women gaze on him. He plodded on, hoping he was not blushing.

"Well, you see, I have this restaurant up there…" he said, waving his too-big arms towards the pier.

The server girl whistled. She looked in her early twenties, her face a perfect oval shape, her hair raised in a neat bun.

"The Kon Tikki? Haven't been there yet, but it looks great!" she said.

"Yes I saw you, yesterday," the woman said in a snide tone. "And you saw me there, too."

He had seen how the men around the mayor had treated her. The Green Crusader, they had called her. And right she looked like one, embittered activist.

"So, I guess you want to know more about the medusa plague?" she said.

He nodded, then remembered the point of his errand.

"Well, yes, that," he said, unsettled by the burning gaze of the tall woman.

Liar, liar, liar! the gulls crossed the sky overhead. Josh refrain from the urge of throwing curses at the flying rats. He turned to the red-haired waitress.

"I came here because I saw you," he said.

Dork, dork, dork! Josh berated himself. He really wished Rafe was here to smooth-talk any opposition.

"Really? Me?" the young woman said, appraising him.

Josh passed one meaty hand over his scalp, belatedly remembered he had no more hair, and let it drop by his side. He drew a breath and spouted out his errand before losing courage.

"Well, what I want to say is, I'm out of staff, the guy I hired quit yesterday without advice, and, well, I need to replace him, and you looked like a perfect candidate..."

He ran out of steam and let the phrase hang, in the salty air and the crush of waves and smell of seaweeds.

"It's nice of you, but I like the place I'm in right now."

Josh's shoulder slumped. The waitress looked away, then perked up.

"Well, mister, if you don't look too hard at experience, I think I have a candidate for you. My bro did some work as a bar server, and he's looking for work."

Josh scanned the beach. The teen with the boombox had drawn near, but he looked too young to be her brother. A young, ripped guy with sunglasses was emptying his garbage bag in one of the bins, its almost-liquid content sloshing in, exhaling a rotting scent mollusk.

The young waitress smiled.

"Oh, Bobbie's not here. He just went with Alan to clean the other end of the beach, past those rocks. You'll recognize him, he has the same hair as mine."

Too happy at the idea of solving his staff problem, Josh thanked her and rushed off, barely hearing the older woman say "but he should get gloves!

13 - A BURIED CHAIN

Disgusting! Rob thought.

He had fished from the packed sand the extremities of a length of iron chain. Rusted by repeated exposition to the air at low tide. It was festooned with algae and ripped plastic, stuck in the holes of the links. The sea did not waste any available space.

He pulled harder to free the rest of the chain, and got six feet off before he met with resistance. The chain, slick with a slurry of microbes, was fastened to something buried under, probably a concrete brick forgotten there. It was light, but strong enough to attach some floating device to it, like a wooden platform or an inflatable boat, both long dead from the look of it.

The family who had set up the anchor had left, and forgotten to retrieve the chain. Kathleen had been wary of the jellyfishes, but the hidden plastic shards, rusted metal and glass chinks were just as dangerous to beach goers walking barefoot.

He pulled out the gloves, passing a weary hand in his

hair. Mel had jauntily announced there would be free pizza at the diner. He wondered about how she would pay for it, if her boss did not agree for the boon. And if she had done it to grant *him* a free meal. It wouldn't be the first time since she worked at the diner, but Rob had skirted the place to avoid her sister getting into troubles on his behalf. Today had been an exception, but he had insisted to pay for his meal.

The water was lapping at his ankles now. Rob put the gloves back, gripped the chain closer to the invisible rock or brick position. He arched his whole body backwards as he heaved with a tree logger's han! The invisible anchor under the sand did not budge.

He steadied his grip, his arms pulled so taut his tendons tingled with pinpoints of pain, but the object had decided to stay there. He heard the surf washing more things on the beach, his toes squishing inside his now damp shoes. But C.A! he was close.

He shook himself, gripped the chain, surprised the links were still so strong despite their worn out aspect. Feet locked apart, Rob pulled on the chain, his back arching, an animal roar rising from his tight throat. The object resisted, but he pulled and pulled, fingers aching, the links grating against his gloves.

And he felt the chain going taut and, incredibly one sand-encrusted link at the time, the chain rose. He redoubled his efforts, grunting with an odd echo, until, with a liquid protest, the chain whipped out, trailing not a brick, but a two-gallon jug filled with cement.

At the moment it was exposed to the light of day, like a metal vampire, the last link broke, sending Rob flying backwards with the shortened chain in his hands.

His back made contact with an unexpected cushion,

warm and firm, covered with cotton fabric. The soggy chain clinked.

"Whoa!" a deep voice said, over his head.

The voice pervaded all over Rob's body with warmth, spreading everywhere.

Maybe he was still in his bed, dreaming. He did not dare open his eyes to find out. But the *caw-caw-caw*! Of a lonely gull and the surf washing his feet brought him to his senses.

His peripheral vision took in a brown arm covered with the blue dragons, the wrist thick as Rob's own arms. He had seen those intricate, sinuous patterns recently.

14 - PULLING HARD

FOR A STUNNED MINUTE, Josh stood transfixed on the rock, not believing what he saw under his feet. The sister had been right about the hair, a flaming orange lit up by the last rays of the setting sun. Josh had not been attentive enough when the young woman had told him the name, otherwise he would have rushed faster over the tongue of fractured rock.

The thin young man from the previous evening was heaving and panting, exerting himself to his physical limits. His lean body traced an graceful arc, his arms taut like ropes, as he pulled a rusted chain off the sand. But the object would not concede victory so easily.

A low growl rising from the throat sent shivers along Josh's spine, who envisioned another kind of grunting. The chain was taut, but slender elf did not stop, his muscles tracing angry lines on his forearms, the skin flushing redder, ever under the graceful wave carrying the boat.

Josh had rarely encountered such dedication to a goal, in the face of unbeatable odds. An indomitable will. The boy's upturned face was turning a deeper shade of red.

Maybe too much dedication? He did not look about to cast the towel. And there had been this insulin problem. That's when Josh noticed the extra length of chain hanging free.

He jumped like a cat, landing on the sand behind the too-involved young man. He grabbed the chain in his bare hands, and heaved. The damn thing was stuck hard, and even their combined forces were barely enough to dislodge the thing.

Then a roar of triumph escaped the young man's lips as the sand fell away from a round, white object. The last chain link snapped, so fast neither Josh nor the elf had the time to check their balance before toppling backwards.

Josh struck the soft sand, a split second before receiving the light body of his future server.

15 - HELP WANTED

Rob was spent, drained and dizzy from his efforts, not in the least hurry to get up from the stranger's lap. Not a stranger: the buried anchor had had no chance at all against this Hercules. From so close, he could spot any individual strand of hair covering the striated forearms laying over his waist.

Tallgate, his name was.

"Thanks, for the assist," he said, letting the chain drop from his grip. "Again," he added, his gaze turned to the sky.

The big warrior shifted his position under Rob, letting the younger man feel the intimacy of the inner legs, the stone-hard muscles of the crossed legs, thick as trees under him. Rob's hair brushed against a hardened chest.

He should get up, but the man seemed no more anxious to release him. Gradually, the exhaustion of his pulling the chain receded, changed for a pervading sense of being safe enclose in those protective arms. He could lay there all afternoon...

The tide decided otherwise.

A powerful wave climbed over the beach, white foam bubbling around them to die against the rock, splashing them copiously in the process.

The two men scrambled up, Josh cursing at his soggy pants, Rob still exhausted from his efforts. Water had seeped in his gloves, and he pulled them off to empty them.

"What are you doing here?" he asked. "Helping out?"

The bald giant shook his head.

"Er, no, I'm the one actually needing help."

Rob blinked.

"What kind of help?" he asked, instantly wary.

If he had a dime for all the guys telling him they needed a special kind of help…

16 - RELIEVING A BURDEN

JOSH TALLGATE CAUGHT the defiant expression on the younger man's face. *Of all the times to be misinterpreted!* he thought. He rose his palms in a placating gesture.

"No, man, it's all legit!" he blurted, backpedaling.

Liar, liar, liar!

Josh shivered. Of course, the flying rats were everywhere. He shot lasers at the white bird who had made a graceful pass over them, noting how the sky was turning into a deeper shade of blue, before returning to the matter at hand.

"Your sister told me where to find you," he added, in a meek voice.

The blue gaze lightened up, all wariness erased.

"You talked to Mel?"

Surging sheet of water lapped their pant legs. The tide was rising. Soon, the whole sandy bar would be submerged.

"Let's get back to the other side," Josh said, lifting one soggy Nike off the damp sand.

He would have to change shoes back at the Tikki.

"Wait a sec," the slender redhead said. "I didn't bust my back here for nothing."

He bent to gather the chain loops in a black garbage bag. It was a messy work with all the threads and algae clinging to each link. Josh helped the younger man wrestle the last parts.

Then, he spotted a vivid splash of yellow brought by the last surf. He peered closer, one hand hovering over the pudding-colored cushion.

"Hey, careful with that!"

Josh turned, to see a look of alarm trembling in the blue, limpid eyes.

"Those jellyfishes sting can be mortal," the fiery-haired elf said.

Josh tapped the yellow dome with the tip of his soaked Nike. The move sent ripples through the gelatinous mass.

"Well," he said, "I know a bit about those. The dangerous part is in the trailing filaments."

His grampa had shown him the most dangerous species, the mortal blue box kind, but he wasn't well-acquainted with the Atlantic species. But he pulled up his foot, not wanting to annoy his prospective employee. Said prospective employee was, at the moment, gazing at Josh's scarred hands.

"She didn't give you gloves?" he asked, his fine orange-brown brows raised in dismay.

"No, uh, I guess I was in a hurry," Josh said, his right hand brushing his non-existent hair. "But I can help carry your other bag."

That chain would be a heavy burden.

"Huh, yes, t'would be nice," Rob said, his blue eyes darting away.

The young man unfolded another black garbage bag from a jean pocket. He disposed the bag downslope from the stranded jellyfish, open. Then he delicately prodded the gelatinous mass, letting gravity roll it inside the opening.

17 - PIZZA NIGHT

ROB FELT the twin prongs of anxiety and desire playing with him as he picked his way over the rounded granitic rock crisscrossed with pale veins, like old scars. When Josh Tallgate had raised his hand to his scalp, the gesture had revealed two scars in a X pattern, not well hidden under the ink. The ink had emphasized Josh's perfect arms into a work of art.

He almost lost his tongue when Josh proposed to carry his bag.

Now, he felt utterly aware of the powerhouse following a scant paces behind him. If he had been walking in a shadowy NY street, Rob would have run as fast as his legs permitted. The kind of hoodlum his mom had warned him against, before he left for college. Ah, the college... *Those years will change you*, she had said, holding him in a tight motherly embrace.

Yes, college *had* changed him, but not in the expected way.

When they jumped from the rock to the dandy area, taking care not to slip on their damp soles, Mel waved happily at them. She had been at work, too, wo-manning the cooler that the cool sunglasses dud had brought, picking scraps in hearing distance of the queen-like woman sitting on his folding chair.

Most of the volunteers were dropping their smelly harvest, and about twenty garbage bags huddled like penguins around the bin-carrying chariot. The gray-haired woman's face was tired, but etched with an odd satisfaction.

"I think we can call it a day," she called out in a strong voice, looking at the huddled bags.

There were no traces left of all the trash that had littered the beach this morning.

He noticed a tall blond man, his eyes etched under sun folds, towering over the seated woman, while the girl in crutches had taken Mel's chair. Rob cast the blond a long glance as he transferred the floppy gelatinous mass from his bag to a metal bin.

However, he found out "calling it a day" still meant getting the penguins-bags to the parking, where a city container waited, attended by eager gulls. Josh and Big Stan volunteered for the task, along with Rob, despite his fatigue.

The two big men heaved the heavy bags as if they were filled with chips, while Rob's seemed filled with more and more gold ingots… But the young man ignored his shoulder and worked on, lifting the bags with the technique he had learned at the store, enjoying the intrigued glances the tattooed warrior-like man cast his way.

In no time, the city waste container was filled to the brim with well-knotted bags, to the despair of the waiting gulls. Rob stretched his shoulders, working out the kinks.

When he returned, the graying lady was rising from his

folding chair, with the careful help of Mel, the girl in crutches watching eagerly.

"I'm buying pizzas at the diner," she announced. "And this young lady even promised one free pizza for everyone who worked on the beach."

She had spoken loud enough for the teen with the boombox to let out a whoop of joy.

"You sure about that, couz?" the blond fisherman asked. "I can help with the check…"

"Pizza looks good for me," Rob said.

Josh looked down at his dirty hands.

"I would love to join you all, but I have left my cook minding the restaurant alone. And besides, I didn't help a lot."

Rob looked up.

"Oh, you certainly helped a lot…," he began, before giving a surprised cry. "Wait a sec, man! You manage a *restaurant*?"

Josh looked at him, startled.

"I own the Kon Tikki," he said. "And yes, we are currently understaffed. I'm short of a waiter, and we're not even talking about hiring an assistant cook. That's the reason I went to see your sis, but she likes where she works and, instead, she pointed me in your direction."

Ha! That was the kind of help he needed, Rob thought. He felt a smile growing on his face at the prospect of seeing more of this intriguing tattooed hunk.

"Well, you're in luck, it seems, 'cause I was searching for a job."

Not wanting to look too smug, Rob quickly added: "Well, I guess, you'll want to interview me, first, to check if I have what you need…," he said, his voice trailing.

The brown warrior brows rose to his scalp, his shoulders straightening as if a weight had been lifted from them. He pointed one thick arm at the overflowing container, and the gulls hacking at the bags. When he smiled, his even teeth shone in his pleasant, chocolate-brown face.

"Mister Rob Sundance," he said, "I don't need an interview. I just saw with my own eyes how hard-working you can be. I think you possess all the qualifications this job requires."

He winked.

"Provided you're not underage," he added.

Rob felt his cheek grow hot. Did he really look seventeen? He felt as worn out as a rag cloth cast under a sink.

His sister smothered a laugh as she folded her chair.

"Mister Tallgate, Bobbie's my *older* brother!"

Josh looked sideways at him, his fleshy lips mouthing a silent *really?* that only Rob saw.

"The pay would be the minimal wage for now," he said, "but subject to negotiations, of course."

Mel insinuated herself between them, the two folding chairs under one arm.

"Any negotiation is better over a hot pizza," she said. "So come another day when you can free yourself."

18 - NEW HIRE

"Where did you find him?" Henry asked in a puzzled voice.

The chef had propped his elbow against the workplan, his ladle propped mid-air over the pot of warming *bouill-abaisse*.

He had been distracted this morning, and his shirt sleeve had taken fire from the front burner of the Ther-midor. Only Rob's quick action with the extinguisher hose had saved the restaurant. Josh had rushed as well, his brow and scalp beaded with sweat. It had taken several seconds for his heart to return to a normal beat, while the young man and the cook examined the damages.

The scent of fresh-cut garlic mixed with the saffron and potatoes suffused the kitchen with a hefty dose of simple earthly happiness that Josh wished his grandad had known. He had done well, so well, - was it only two days before? – to go for fresh fishes. The scampi, red mullet, haddock, halibut, cod, and various shell fishes rested on a bed of ice in the freezer, to be pulled at need. The complex

Provençal broth required a full day of prepping, before advancing on the rouille sauce.

"Let's say I found him inside a closet," Josh said, smiling inwardly.

Henry was too straight and uptight to guess at the irony.

"Is it acceptable, this way?" Henry's new assistant asked, proffering a plate of neatly cut vegetables. "I diced those the way you asked."

Josh cast one exerted eye on the Yukon potatoes and the mid-west celery. Rob had taken too at heart the one-inch instruction about the celery, each lineated morsel of a similar length, as of cut by a machine. The potatoes were cut in a similar fashion, the center cut in perfect one half-inch cubes.

"You're certain you never worked in a restaurant?" Henry asked the young man.

Rob lifted one gloved hand to his head, before remembering that his hair was under the bonnet. He wore a white apron and a working shirt with long sleeves tapering to the wrists, so no swath of fabric would get in the way of great cooking.

"Well, I did help my mother when I was a kid. She always had trouble cutting the vegetables or lettuce or whatever needed peeling, cutting, dicing. She would take three times the magazine's theoretical time."

"I see," Henry said, pulling at his short mustache. "Well, lad, I really appreciate you taking the time to help me."

And Josh did, too. Even if Rob's official designation was as server, and Josh hadn't looked a the boy's papers yet to officialize the hiring.

In the morning, there were few people at the pier, and

the young recruit had quickly grown bored of chasing the gulls away from the tables he had just set. So, the young man had proposed to assist the cook.

And Josh saw no problem, except when the first clients came in, and the white assistant-cook stripped to his dark pants and tee, donned a dark belt-purse from the bar, and a pad. The rising light of the sun set Rob's flaming hair; and Josh suddenly found difficult to concentrate on his own management. He had been passing a cloth over the inox copper surface, pressing so hard he created a perfect clean spot on the counter.

He bent and touched the smooth top of the titanium safe, anchored to the metal shelf under the counter he had inherited from the former owner. The conspicuous black-sided cash gilded with gold register sat on one end, unused. Josh would have to replace the thing with the latest electronic payment system, but for now he managed to pass credit cards with his own phone and a *Moneyfast* application.

Josh never had to manage money before, and the opening day had been an eye-opener to his lack of people management skills. He missed Rafe, who had a knack to make paying the addition an intimate favor. He surmised he had lost at least nine or ten meal's worth in that horrid day.

Nevertheless, he thought, following the redhead as he scrubbed a peculiar spot from a table, *I have found a rare pearl*. His insides shivered at the word.

Only once had he used those words, and it had not ended well.

Rob had told him he had worked in a bar, laying to rest Josh's fear that he was underage. Josh played with the idea of letting the young man manage the bar. His hand brushed the top of the steel safe beside the tiny sink. Here were the sum of his dreams, collected along years of hard work.

Liar! Liar! Liar!

And from the insurance settlement after the fire.

"Hey, get off there, shoot!"

Rob's voice had a joyful edge to it, as if he was playing catch with the birds. He was waving a table cloth at the fiends, shooing them away with a youthful energy that belied his years. He had found out the young sprite age, and still reeled from the realization that only five years separated them.

Rob was having a staring contest with an older, all-white gull. The bird lifted his wings and soared away.

"I can't believe you're 27," he said, in a playful voice.

"Huh," the young man said.

"Like Kurt Cobain's age when he took his own life," Henry said, emerging from the kitchen's swiveling door. "Lots of celebs died at that age," he added with a somber tone.

Josh frowned. The chef was about the age Kurt C. would have been, had he lived. Not a great improvement.

The young man folded back the cloth he had used to chase the birds.

"It's only a law of great numbers," Rob said. "There are as much death at any age. And we're on a planet with eight billion individuals. Just the probabilities would indicate that…"

Then, the elf noticed how Josh *and* Henry were staring at him.

"Well, the age thing is not significative," he finished in a subdued, hurried voice.

Josh had a fleeting impression of a good student who

didn't want to shine too brightly in front of the class bullies.

The impression faded when an impish grin came back on the elf's lips.

"Same for me, boss," he said. "I can't believe you're only 32!"

Then, the young man scampered away on boundless energy, to greet the first clients.

Henry turned gravely to Josh.

"Boss, tell me," he said, his gruff voice playful this time.

"Where the *heck* did you find him?"

19 - MONDAY'S PIXIE GIRL

THE PIER WAS STILL CALM at this time, a Monday morning, when many people would be touring, or working, or leaving. Rob had found Henry already onsite, preparing the meals that needed TLC, and cursing against the Thermidor's weird controls.

He hoped his second day at the restaurant would go as well as his first. He found Henry and his bushy mustache grumpy at first, but since the burnt sleeve incident, the older man had relented.

Rob was walking out of the kitchen with new fabric-packaged sets of utensils to lay on the table when he heard his name called.

"Hey, Rob!"

He looked at, the young close-cropped woman in crutches, her chin barely reaching over the bamboo railing separating the terrace from the promenade level.

He grinned and waved back.

"Hey, you," he said. "Want to rest a little?"

Rob had done it at the hardware store, too and that

had not gone very well. Suddenly he turned to his boss, searching for his approval.

Josh shrugged from the bar.

"It's not like we have tons of clients right now!" he said.

The morning had been slow going. He hoped the nice old couple would come back.

The girl with crutches – Maeve, Rob recalled -- sat awkwardly at the table by the promenade, leaning the crutches on the railing. She was sweating, her hair damp.

Rob was quick to bring her a glass of water, with ice cubes tinkling.

"Oh, you should not bother, I just needed to rest my legs."

"Non sense," Rob said. "It's hot, and water is free."

At least, I think *we don't charge for water,* he thought. He cast a look at his boss, for confirmation. Josh grinned and stepped closer to the table.

"And how is our, ahem, 'dangerous green crusader'?" he asked, mimicking the commas with his free hands. "Or our beach general?"

Maeve's lips twitched in an amused smile.

"Oh, don't call her that way," she said. "Kathleen drove out of town for a meeting."

"Where?" Josh asked, his brow knotting.

The young woman thought for a moment.

"I think she spoke of Fallsworth, north of here," she said. "A public consultation about some fracking project."

Oh brother! Rob thought. *Our tax dollars at work!*

At college, he had seen some collective protest against the destruction of a well-loved patch of forest. There had been some "consultations", but it seemed to the young man that the only opinions that mattered where that of the promoters. He had been expelled before seeing the condo-minium towers rising there. And now, the Fallsworth project.

"Scratch the 'public'," Rob said. "The announcement on the public boards and the Net came so late nobody had time to prepare a memoir."

Josh and Maeve looked up at him, puzzled.

"What's a memoir?" the two said in unison.

"Well, in short, it's a document, a letter that you write detailing your preoccupation, I mean, the problem that concerns you and the ways it affects you…"

As Rob explained, his hands flying as he talked, Josh clapped his skull.

"I hired a genius," he said.

Henry was right, Josh thought, amused. *I hired an fricking genius.*

Rob had blushed like a girl under his orange hair, which made his freckles stand out on his pale skin. Josh had learned his server had not finished college, but read a lot.

"As long as you don't read on the job!" Josh had said, giving a light tap on his server's shoulder.

Now, he watched the young man and the girl talking, looking like any hetero couple. He did his best not to eaves-drop but, as there was a lull in clients, he strode back to their table to share in the conversation .

It had been a while since Josh could just sit there and talk with a young woman. Something in her open eyes drew people to confide; Rob had been opening himself, like a dirty-grained oyster revealing a pristine pearl inside.

At a point, Josh smelled the scent of overcooked fish, and a curse sounded from the kitchen.

"Better go see if Henry's not putting the place on fire," he said.

Rob up and went, sauntering, and soon, Josh heard his calm voice taming the cook's burr.

"He looks happier here than at the Tool Barn."

Josh turned to the cropped-haired woman. She had a oddly familiar face, but he could not replace her. She wore a black *Dr Who* Tee.

"You can say that!" he said, with a short bark.

He had seen up close how Rob's life had been there.

The young woman looked at him, probably intrigued by his markings. Josh returned the gaze. The young woman had an eager pixie-like face, oddly familiar.

"So, Mister, er…," she began, then let her voice trail.

"Josh Tallgate."

"I'm Maeve. What did bring you here to open a restaurant?"

More intrigued than upset by the directness of the question, Josh paused, gazing at the blue cabin on the pixie's Tee-shirt.

What if she were a reporter, or an investigative journalist? He had much to lose, despite his precautions. But he sensed no more than honest curiosity from her. So he settled for a generality not too far from the truth.

"Cause my last place got torched by the mob," he said.

The shock, on her face.

"I'm sorry," she said.

"Nothing to be done about it. There were like twenty-four shops and restaurants burnt to embers the same month. I don't miss the city."

Again, she gave him a long, far away look.

"So you left, and came here," she said.

He pause in his fidgeting.

"For the air, and the sea. And the best thing..."

He smiled.

"No protection racket or mob here!"

At this moment, Josh saw a young couple checking the menu hanging at the post. Both were unusually handsome in the way of the twenty-something could be. Young actors, maybe? Then he recognized the ripped guy from the beach cleaning, and his girlfriend as they hopped the stairs to the terrace.

He rose in a fluid motion to greet his first afternoon clients. By the time he had installed the couple, Maeve and her crutches were gone. Only an empty glass of water remained as proof of her passage.

20 - QUIET TUESDAY

THE WOMAN HAD a cloud of white hair and a pastel sweater rising high enough to protect her neck. Her doting husband used a cane to steady himself as he grabbed the bamboo railing.

Rob, who had been shooing away a too-eager gull, hurried to help them negotiating the two stairs to the terrace. He sat them close to the kitchen bamboo wall with the picture, to get the clients out of the sun. Rob felt sorry in his mind for the wheelchair-bound people who could not get up here. Accessibility had not been huge at the time of the former *Mama* restaurant. Nor had it been for the other elevated terraces on the Pier.

Rob promised himself to check the Safe Harbor regulations, and to see what would be required to build an access ramp.

Then he handed them the thick, glossy menus Josh had had printed out. The menus were thick and big as a tabloid sheet, with vivid pics of sea animals in various poses of death (not the client's opinion) that garnered the plates.

"I remember that picture. Do you, dear?"

The nice lady with the pastel sweater and cloud-like hairdo had come back to eat at the Kon Tikki. The husband squinted at the gray 11x14 inches enlarged print on the bamboo-strewn wall, framed in a similar tainted wood. Seven pale-haired, pale skinned men grinned at a camera. All white guys, heteros for sure, but in 1947, that was to be expected. War had just ended, and humanity needed to turn at a positive endeavor.

"My God, I was just a kid then," the elderly man said, waving his menu in a circle that would have caught Rob if he had not stepped back.

"It must have been quite a feat," he said. "May I take your order? The plat du jour is a *bouillabaisse*."

"Oooh, really?" Mrs. Porter said, elated.

In the two days, the young man had found his groove and become at ease with the clients, whose names he strived to learn, and the menu, which he knew by heart.

Rob had noticed the portrait hanging over the bamboo wall on his first day at the restaurant. And had searched the Web in his down times.

The original Kon-Tiki had been an experiment in migration routes led by the now-famous Thor Heyerdahl, who contended that humans had the means to travel large distances by seas.

Thor Heyerdahl had the raft built in balsa wood. Balsa had the peculiarity of being soft for the cords binding the shafts together. The cables gradually burrowed in the soft wood, augmenting their protection.

Their voyage had been fraught with dangers and practical problems, like, how to keep drinking water from spoiling? How to refresh one's feet in the sea without getting chomped by the omnipresent sharks? How to cook flying fishes fallen on the boat? How to protect the big sail from harm?

He had pored over the black-and-white pics of the expedition. All sunny pics, none taken while the crew was furling the main sail in a storm, or clinging to the ropes when the small embarkation coasted house-sized waves.

"Where's the name come from?"

Mrs. Porter asked, cleaning the corner of her mouth with a fabric napkin.

"It's an older name of the Inca God Viracocha," Rob said.

"But why take a Inca God?" Mrs. Porter asked.

Rob had an answer ready.

"Because Mr. Heyerdahl had wanted to prove that Incas could have sailed from the coat of south America to settle the Polynesian islands, long before Columbus discovered the Americas, about 1200 AD."

"It boggles the mind to think primitive men could sail such a distance, so long ago."

"And women, dear, women, too, otherwise they couldn't make babies! How long did it take?" she added.

"Oh, they did well, in four months," Rob said. "The Kon-Tiki got to Tuamotus island in the Samoas."

He caught Josh smiling at him from the bar, like a proud father. His heart leapt up as he walked into the kitchen. It was a joy for Rob to be around the big hunk but, since the beach episode, the tall man had not made any overture. Anyway, they would have to behave in public. In the secret of his room, Rob would curl up and let his imagination run wild…

He gave the slip of paper with the order to Henry, then he returned outside with glasses of water for the Porters.

When he stole a glance at the warrior, Josh was still

tinkering at the bar, but his absent gaze was levelled at the horizon.

Rob had soon found out that his boss had *moments*.

Moments when he would hand out the menus, and suddenly his gaze would fly over the heads of the clients, to the flatlined ocean, as if he had seen some captivating thing. Or he would frown at the hovering birds, the blood darkening his temples along with the ink. And he always sniffed out the air in alarm at the least burnt odor, whether coming from Henry's adventures with the Thermidor stove, or from another shop.

His usual station at the elevated bar counter gave him a splendid view of the sea and the beach. Rob surprised his boss scanning the crowd, the white of his eyes betraying his edge.

Rob's overactive mind would conjure various scenarios.

But what could he be afraid of, in quaint Safe Harbor?

THEN, his attention was taken up by a massive blond man, his face familiar, walking up the steps to the terrace.

The blond fisherman sat close to the bamboo railing, his orange tee reeking of sweat and fish. He remembered him from the "beach party", as the lady's big nephew.

"Big day today," Rob said.

"Huh-huh."

He looked exhausted.

"Stanley, is it?" Rob asked. "You were at the beach cleaning the other day."

"Guilty as charged. And you must be Rob. Maeve told me you got a job here."

He smiled, despite the weariness, his hands leaving smudges on the table.

"Sorry," he said, I should get to the loos and…"

"Nonsense, we have damp towels here," Rob said.

He retreated, aware of the heat building up inside him. The blond Viking-like man was attractive. Only the thought of young Maeve, obviously in love, and his hunky boss, whose dark eyes were on him, prevented Rob from brushing by. He snatched a couple of baby-moist towels from the kitchen, and came back with the glossy menu, handing both to Stanley.

The fisherman ordered the *mets du jour*, and everything proceeded smoothly, except when Josh came by to chat.

Josh had an excellent memory and called Stanley by his name.

"So, Mr. Marchand, I see you're working on the blue boat," he said. "Is it something mechanic?"

Rob, coming and serving, could not avoid wondering how good Josh was with people. Besides Stanley, he had treated each diner as his personal guests.

Even when a black-clad couple found out they did not have enough to pay for the whole dinner, Josh treated the goth-style women as royalties, and bade them to return. Used to the New-York seedier joints, Rob would have asked to see their plastic cards or given them hell.

Stanley did not mind talking. Most clients had left, and Rob caught much of the conversation while picking up empty plates, before the gulls beat him to it.

Fish captures had dwindled so much Stanley had had to go farther and farther to catch something else that jelly-fishes. So he had decided to convert his boat to offer water tours. At some point in the season there would be whales and dolphins to be observed, and otherwise the coast and birds offered plenty to see.

Rob had never been near whales in real life, not even in aquariums. He would love to get the occasion to see the big beasts up close and, maybe, to touch them.

"Your aunt, Ms. Marchand, is concerned about the jellyfishes," Josh was saying. "When she came at the opening, the mayor called her the Green Crusader. She was, er, very driven."

The big man's gaze dropped to his half finished plate.

"She lost her daughter to those things. My cousin."

So this explains the haunted look in the nice lady's eyes, Rob thought, remembering the beach cleaning.

"Oh man, I'm so sorry, I didn't know!" Josh said.

"It was a long time ago," Stanley said, his voice dragging the ocean bottom.

21 - WEDNESDAY'S WORRIES

THE AGE of his server out of the way, Josh hoped to build a tentative friendship.

No, it would be more than a friendship: his fingers itched to grab the thin shoulders, pass one hand on the red waves of hair, trace the delicate jaw with a finger. He experienced potent reveries in the night that left him panting and sweating in his apartment bed.

Not only was the boy older, he was knowledgeable, and curious, with a wealth of culture. Even if Rob told him he looked it up on the internet,

When he had heard Rob explaining about the Kon-Tiki expedition, Josh had felt elation. It had been a wonderful moment. The red-haired elf had a knack for being outgoing, and put people at ease.

He followed with this eyes the slim back of his new server as Rob rushed inside the kitchen.

Then, his attention returned to the yellow slip of paper in his hands. He had found the slip on the counter's surface, stuck under a heavy pebble so the wind would not carry it away.

In the message, three words.

You Owe Us.

No! Josh thought. He owed nothing! The insurance money…

A gull flapped by, a fish in his bill, two others flying behind in hot pursuit.

Liar, liar!

Josh crumpled the slip between his fingers, while his spirit crumbled, too. If a tourist stepped up the terrace for a drink, he would be unable to take the order, much less preparing it.

"Hey."

Josh almost jumped out of his skin. Rob was hunched over the counter on his forearms, his blue eyes filled with concern. Had he seen the slip of paper in his hands?

"Is there something I can do? You look as if you just saw a ghost."

Josh instantly tensed, then he forced himself to relax his grip on the crumbled ball of paper. He pushed it in a pocket of his black apron, under the counter, keeping his eyes on Rob's elfish face.

"N-nothing," he said, turning to look at the horizon.

The quaver in his voice screamed at 110 decibels in Josh's anguished mind.

Rob's wonderful eyes followed his gaze towards the promenade, the beach, the rock, the sea. The weather forecast that Josh dutifully listened every morning at six had promised a beautiful day, meaning he would get eating clients.

"I'm fine," he added, on a more even tone, hoping his server's keen attention would gloss over it.

No gulls passed overhead, for which Josh felt inordinately grateful.

22 - LONELY GULL

Using a long pair of tweezers, Rob retrieved a bread crumb stuck on burner number three of the Thermidor range. Starting the flames would have ignited the dry bread, the smoke would have touched the captors of the white pill screwed on the ceiling. The fire alarm screech would have shocked the clients, scattering off any incoming stroller, and forced Henry or him to step on a rickety chair to stop it.

And adding one more worry for his boss. Yesterday, Josh had looked like a stranger, his evasive answers a clear signal not to prod further.

Rob deposited the brown cube on the work surface. Henry shrugged.

"Food for the flying rats," he said.

Rob palmed the hard brown cube.

There was one window at the back of the kitchen, overlooking the narrow quay of the marina. A solitary gull was hunched on a post, immobile as a statue, probably sleeping, its orange legs under him. The bird had taken station there, for the three days of Rob's service.

For a flying rat, he looks pretty good, Rob thought. An adult in his mature, white plumage, with the slate gray back.

Rob pushed the window open and leaned out, the corrugated edge of the slanted roof inches from his head. He understood why most of the restaurants and shop had not built terraces on the south side of the elevated pier.

First, the midday sun was drilling fire in his eyes. Then, the long arm of the concrete wave breaker shut off the horizon. He would have to stand at the top of Old Man's rock to see it. The string of white yachts was fun to look at, but anyone could walk to the end of the pier to get a full view.

He threw the dried-out bread in the gull's direction.

The bird had been sleeping in appearance only. Before the brown cube had flown half of the arc toward it, the gull flapped its wings. It jumped high, its dark-circled beak already open wide, then closing on the target with the natural ease of a goal keeper catching the ball at a soccer game.

The bird returned to its perch. As it landed, extending its orange legs, Rob blinked in surprise. The bird would have been undistinguishable from thousands of others, if not for its one missing foot. One orange leg terminated with a webbed foot, the other stopped past the ball-shaped knee joint.

How it had lost its foot, Rob had no idea. But that bird had taken station on the post, probably unable to fly far and get his food.

The gull broke the bread in one clicking, then gobbled the fragments. Then it let out a victorious *har-har-har!* before settling down on the post's flat head.

"I think I'll call you Goalie," Rob said.

Rob wondered if the amputated bird was too old to

dive in the waters, or battle more vindictive gulls to get its food.

Law of nature, his dad would have said.

He felt the familiar outrage ran through him at the recollection.

LITTLE ROB HAD ALWAYS loved animals, and he would take in baby birds, their squirming bodies in his hands, to the stupefaction of his little sister.

His mother had done her best to cope with his habit, providing water, grains, Kleenexes. In winter, he would place a wounded bird on the floor grid to warm its small body. But his dad did not share any Disnean feeling.

When Rob had been eight, he had place a wrapped-up chickadee, its black head looking around in alarm from its cocoon of napkins, over a heating grid. Then he had dutifully gone to sleep.

In the morning, he had stumbled downstairs to check on his patient.

The grid was empty, the chickadee gone. Rob found the remnants of the cocoon in the kitchen's wastebasket. Was it healed? The little boy had ran all over the house, listening for a out-of-place chirping.

Then, as he looked over their snow-covered backyard, he had spotted the black and white head over the motionless body. Rob had rushed out in his slipper to take it, but the bird was frozen over, its wings half outstretched, as if the creature had tried to escape its fate.

When he had re-entered the kitchen, he had crossed his mother's sad gaze over her coffee cup. Little four-year-old Mel on her high-chair was following everything, her mouth agape. Before Rob could ask his mom what happened, his father stepped in, clothed and ready to leave for work.

"Why did you put my bird out?" he asked, his child's voice piping up. "He died."

His dad cast a hard look at him, then at his mom.

"Roxanne, you're coddling that boy, he's getting soft as a marshmallow," he said, filling up his traveling coffee mug.

His mom pursed her lips in a thin line.

His dad turned to Rob, standing upright, his damp slippers leaking meltwater on the tiles. Black and white tiles, like the chickadee's head.

"That bird was wounded, it couldn't have survived on its own. So I ended its sufferings."

"But," Rob had protested.

His dad's gaze was frozen.

"It's the law of nature, boy. The strong survive, the weak don't. Same for humans. I work my head off to get food on that table."

The first sliver of discontent pointed in the little boy's heart. Something was wrong with his dad. Not with him.

"I wanted to heal it before letting him go," Rob insisted. "He would have gotten a second chance…"

His voice trailed off under his dad's anger.

"A second chance? There's no such thing in our world!"

"Why, now you're getting overboard, Don," his mom said. "He's compassionate, that's all."

"Compassion? In the real world, he'll get gobbled up with his compassion!"

Rob did not remember their parents heated exchanges after, because tears blurred out everything. He did not remember the soggy cereals in his bowl or how his chocolate milk tasted. He vaguely heard his dads' angry footsteps receding down the hall, the front door slamming shut.

"ROB?" a voice asked.

Not Henry's.

Rob went back to himself, hunched over the windowsill, hot tears streaming down his chin and falling, the wind dispersing them. He brushed his eyes with one hand before turning back.

Josh was standing next to the metal fridge, the half-opened door doubling his brown head. He held a red bottle of ketchup in one meaty hand.

"You OK, man?" the two heads asked.

Rob swallowed the sad memories.

"Yeah," he lied. "I'm OK."

Josh closed the steel door.

"If you need your insulin, or to rest, you tell me."

The caring in the low tone brought Rob's mood around. He smiled.

"I'm OK," he said again. "Just a bad memory."

Henry was looking at them, a ladle in hand, a twitch in his gray mustache.

"Do we all have those," he said, with a sad overtone, before returning to wage his war on the Thermidor.

Rob looked at Josh, then at the cook cursing at a half-cooked fish on a pan.

"Where did you find *him*?" he asked.

His big warrior smiled, for the first time in the day. It was as if the sun had evaporated Rob's woes. Josh had returned to his formidable self.

"If I told you, you wouldn't believe me," he said.

23 - FREAKY FRIDAY

THE NEXT DAY, Rob had decided to get up early. In the night, among his dreams, an idea to protect the tables from the birds had arisen in his mind. He wanted to try it out before either Josh or Henry came in. He walked on the wooden promenade, relishing the quiet of the morning.

The pier looked still and empty, except for the anglers at the very end, their canes, hair-thin in the distance, stretched out.

Presently they were packing, bending over cases and zipping their fishing gear in bags. Their path crossed Rob's in front of the fine arts shop at the middle of the pier. The men looked younger than the geezers Rob had seen the week before, tanned and well-built. Probably veterans, in search of some peace, their eyes obscured by their long-bill caps.

The young man smiled inwardly at the conversation of the previous day. That had thawed the ice remaining between Henry and Rob.

Henry was a old curmudgeon, twice divorced with a brood of grown up kids that he never saw. *I'm not really the father type*, he had said after another battle with the Thermidor. Then his whiskers lit up with a wicked smile as a scantily-clad woman passed on the narrow quay under the window.

So Rob was grinning as he stepped jauntily over the stairs, pushing with his hands on the short bamboo railings, like an athlete.

He examined the terrace. No birds had decorated the empty tables yet, but as soon as they put something on them, even wrapped utensils and ketchup bottles, an army of eager gulls would circle over the terrace. When the hot plates coming out from the kitchen, there would be a battle.

Rob examined the orange nets stretched on the bamboo strew wall and the high posts marking the corners of the square. He pulled on one, slick on his fingers, and with a heaviness of hard plastic. Real fishing net, discarded, some part of the orange faded out by the sun. He tried to pull apart two lozenge-holes, without success. There was a thing to be said for authenticity and solidity, but the weight of this net would make it hang too low. And some old odors were still embedded in the plastic.

Rob could find a very flimsy net, almost invisible, that could be stretched high enough over the heads so no one would accidentally touch it, without giving the impression of an orange cage. There had been some nice ones at the Tool Barn... His hands cramped. He would not return there, even as a client.

It was as he pondered the possibility of asking his sexy boss for a jaunt to the other city, he noticed something amiss on the terrace. His eyes roamed the tall posts, the bamboo covered wall at the back...

There. On the wall over the best table, two nails

protruded among the bamboo slats.

The Kon-Tiki photo with the crew had been removed.

Forgetting his nets idea, Rob looked wildly around him. The solid door of the kitchen was closed, as was the bar counter, all liquors safely stored in locked cupboards. Only Josh had the key, and he was always onsite when Rob came in.

But the nice picture had been hanging in full view, unprotected. Some bored teenager had stolen it, probably for the kick, since so few people knew about Thor Heyerdahl and his crew accomplishment. The picture had been printed on glossy photo paper. It could be replaced, and the frame, too…

Something cracked under his basketball shoe. Rob lifted his foot, looked down: fragments of very thin glass, like the pane covering the pic. He crouched to look under the tables and chair legs: more brilliant, angular fragments reflected the light, along with bits of straight wood. The wood still had indentations of the small nails holding the cord.

So.

The bored teenager had smashed the frame and made out with the picture. Stupid: the wooden frame was probably more expensive than the print itself.

Rob remembered how he himself had been, after his dad had sent him at a private boarding school, to "toughen him up". How he would smash things there, get into fights despite his size, just to get a tiny measure of control over his life. He got expelled, sent to another place, and eventually he took his mom's advice and found solace in books.

He walked over the terrace. As he came facing the bar, he saw that the little flap that let the barman in was laying against the counter, leaving the bar enclosure open.

This was exclusive Josh territory, without any chair or high stool, the built-in tiled floor free of anything that would hinder the barman. The spigots for water jutted like silver swan's necks over the small sink. The ice machine and four cubic feet fridge would be under the counter. The cupboards and their variously shaped bottles were stacked against the mirror. It was not a real mirror like in western movies, when everyone had to watch their back, but a thin sheet of brushed aluminum that reflected Rob's haggard face.

The first thing he saw of the damage was the liquor shelf, that held vintage bottles, their reflection doubled. Josh had to protect the bottles against bird depredation, but he hadn't counted with human depredation. Not a single bottle remained on the shelf. The glass doors had been smashed, probably using a six-pound hammer sold at the Tool Barn.

He rounded the bar, to look inside the enclosure.

The lower steel cupboards where Josh locked the beers packs and wine bottles had held fast, despite the hammering that dinked their false wood surface. Josh had told him as he came in the first day how he had bought the best quality apparel for the bar, and how the locks were prime.

Same for the Kleenex-box safe under the counter, its gray steel surface bearing marks. The thing was fixed to the counter structure so not even a tornado could take it away. The last evening's earnings were untouched, waiting to be transferred in the Kon Tikki business account.

As he bent to get a better look at the safe, and fridge, he heard the crystalline crush under his shoes. And looked down.

Oh, *Cee-Ayy*!

The six square feet or so of tiles were littered with irregular glass fragments, all sharp angles pointing to the roof. Rob raised his eyes to the suspended rack: all the graceful champagne flutes, the long goblets, the ball-shaped wine glasses, the conical Martini glasses, the bell-shaped beer glasses, had been pulled out. The teenager, or teenagers, Rob couldn't imagine a sole individual would have had the patience, had smashed the delicate glasses against the hard edge of the counter. They couldn't unlock the fridge, but they had torn the ice machine from its niche in the door: half melted ice cubes lay among the glass shards, with a pack of napkins irreverently dropped in the mess.

He looked around in dismay. What if the bored teenagers, plural, had breached the kitchen? He thought of the window at the back, but there was no way to know for sure without the key to the door. He would have to wait for Josh.

Something tapped the counter behind him. Rob whirled in alarm, the cut glass crunching under his soles. He hadn't seen anyone crouching behind a chair, impossible on this terrace.

Sad, sad! Sad, sad!

A long gull, white, had landed on the counter, folding its wings. Its lone webbed foot was splayed against the counter's copper.

"Oh, hi Goalie," he said. "If only you could talk."

The gull hopped on its remaining leg, avoiding the scattered glass fragments. It opened its bill on a red pointed tongue.

Sad, sad, sad.

"Sorry, boy, or girl, but I can't feed you right now."

24 - VANDALS

THE MORNING LOOMED, full of promises, as Josh walked the three miles distance from his flat to the pier. He had taken a slate-gray cotton hoodie for the fresh early-morning air, but the exercises warmed him. He could have pulled up the hoodie, but he was wary.

He could have bought a used car, but he didn't want his driving license to register. When he really needed to go somewhere for his errands, he used one of the Safe Harbor's three or so taxicabs.

He was off a clean slate, and nothing from his NY period remained of him. He had a pre-paid cell that he managed to rarely use. He had always hid his tattoos under long sleeves when he was a chef, the hairnet holding his dark mane. Very few had known about his inked dragons, except Rafe.

Rafe.

Raphael Giordani, supporter of fine arts, daring entrepreneur, lover extraordinaire... He grabbed his arms through the thick gray fabric.

The pain had receded to a dull ache, like a missing limb. Josh couldn't believe his friend would had taken a loan from sharks. Rafe had said the loan was legit. Beside, his family was old money, not to worry. Josh had not seen anything besides his silver-haired gentleman's face, so different from his own wild looks (but those same wild looks had drawn the gentleman to him in the first place).

Rafe's grinning face floated around him as he walked down main street, then took Ocean Avenue to the pier's parking. He noted that Henry's old Westphalia was parked at its usual place, the rust dots slowly gaining on the burnt orange paint. Two years ago, at the top of his gastronomical fame, Josh would have gladly bought a new car for the man, without even touching his reserves.

Now, Rafe's death had taught him to be prudent with money handling.

He walked the three hundred meters of the promenade that, if the day held its promises, would get his place a flood of tourists. He passed the art and craft tourist trap and a series of shops that were still closed, as was the other restaurant.

Most of the shops open at midday. He had decided they would open at ten, getting the morning crowd with the new coffee maker, while Henry prepared the *plat du jour* for the midday crowd.

A flock of gulls passed over the pier, coasting on extended wings, blessedly silent.

As he neared the Kon Tikki, Josh was greeted by Henry's shouting and Rob's pleading. What was the problem? Henry had the key to the kitchen, so he could start earlier.

Then, he heard a third interlocutor on the premises.

Liar, liar, liar!

From the steps of his terrace, he saw Rob, his expressive hands flying as he argued with Henry. The cook's face was red with indignation, his voice grating in a worrisome way. Henry was not a young man anymore, despite his gusto.

But the more surprising thing was to see a *flying rat* perched on his counter, harking as if it was part of the conversation. The thing was hopping on his counter, if that wasn't aggravating enough.

Josh crossed the terrace, his steps echoing on the wooden floor. The red and gray heads swiveled in unison, something that would have him laugh if it was for their downturned mouths. What was going on here, beside the damnable bird standing on his counter on... *one* leg?

Then his gaze focused on the devastation of the bar around the bird.

Something cold seeped in his bones, made of all the *I-told-you-so* his subconscious had sent to his brainstem, since the opening of the Lucky Traveler, so long ago.

The *I-told-you-so* congealed into a flurry of *I-should-have*. I should have asked Rafe about the loan. I should not have let his devastating smile steer me off-chart. I could have done something to prevent the fire, I should have paid more attention to the snippets of conversation falling around Rafe's table...

Josh remembered explaining the subtleties of the *plat du jour,* clad in his full tuxedo, in a midst of angry murmurs.

Man, that's too daring...

... have to pay back, someday.

And what about the family?

Josh's fists balled in the kangaroo pocket of his slate

gray hoodie, pulling the collar down, the rigid label brushing his nape. He had grown attached to the brushed-cotton sweater, a gift from Rafe, offered three months before the end. "You look like a teen in this," he had said, his rumbling voice caressing the young man's ears as well as his fingers.

He felt his whole body shivering at the recollection. No, never would he hold this wonderful older bod' in his arms, nor pass his fingers in the wavy silver mane. And never will he hear Rafe's voice again.

He became conscious of the two employees staring at him. The kitchen door was opened. What damage waited there? Henry stood in the entrance, Rob next to the bar's opening.

Josh pulled out his hands from the pockets. The air was warming up with the sun rising up, but he was still cold inside.

"Has the kitchen been broken in?" he asked.

Just the new equipment there was worth sixty thousands.

"No, the door was intact," Henry said. "I just went it to check. Nothing stolen."

Josh made one mechanical step toward the bar. He put one hand on the counter to steady himself.

"Bunch of hooligans!" Henry muttered.

"They broke everything that could be broken, then made out with a print of the original Kon-Tiki?" Rob said, his tattooed arm pointing at the empty bamboo wall. "I can't believe it!"

Empty of the print picture Rafe had given him, as the older man pored over his picture book, in the middle of the posh apartment they had shared on the 24th avenue.

He swallowed his sadness. He couldn't let his employees know about the threats. They didn't have to taste the darkness that had plagued him since a few days.

"I agree it must have been a random act of vandalism," Josh said, but his voice sounded mushy to his own ears.

Liar, liar, liar!

He whirled to the one-legged bird hopping on the counter, providing a convenient outlet for the frustration building up inside him.

"What is this thing doing there?"

Rob had shown zeal when chasing off the birds. But the young man's gaze did not waver from him.

"You should call the police," he said. "This was a breaking and entering. We haven't touched anything."

Henry's foot pushed around fragments of broken glass.

"Yeah for the breaking part," he said. "We can count ourselves lucky that they didn't manage to get into the kitchen."

Josh glanced again at the door, closed. He shook his head. He couldn't drag the authorities' attention on him now. They would find more than they bargained for. He and his wallet had sweet-talked the mayor into getting an alcohol permit without the usual red tape.

"No. This was a gratuitous destruction. We will have to close for the day. Clean up the broken glass. I'll buy new glasses and get going tomorrow. Take the day off today. You've earned it, Henry."

Giving a string of directives made Josh feel marginally better.

He had barked commands and instructions to the cooks working in the ballroom-sized kitchen of the Lucky Traveler. Him, barely graduated from the Culinary Institute, Josh had landed a first job in a small kitchen, before Rafe plucked him off and set him up in this prodigious workplace.

A workplace that was burned to the ground, he reminded himself.

25 - KEEPING SILENT

ROB COULD NOT BELIEVE what his big hunk of a boss had said. Now, Josh was giving orders so they get the place cleaned up and working. As if nothing had happened.

Keeping quiet about this incident? His shoulders tensed. He had a fair idea of the kind of idle bums who could have done this. The same that had beaten him and locked him at the tool Barn.

"But what if they do it again?" Rob asked, his arms chopping the air. "Vandalizing another shop?"

Josh's eyes didn't meet his own. His lips parted to say something, then he pressed them together, as if he had thought better of it. Then he turned to the still-pacing gull.

"Shoo!" he said, taking one step, waving his thick arms.

Goalie gave no indication of being impressed. The gull let out a short *kwak*. Then he flexed one golf ball-sized knee, the footless one following the move, and flapped off, supremely indifferent.

Henry cast a glance at the flying bird, then scratched his balding head.

"Nice to give us the day, but I don't like it."

Rob felt the same unease.

"You should at least signal the crime," he said.

The big man's head whipped up, so fast his hood fell back. His brow glistened with beads of sweat.

"This is my restaurant," he said. "My decision. I am not calling the cops."

Josh's voice had taken a hard edge as he spoke. His eyes darkened under his brows. Under the thick cotton fabric, Rob could almost palp the tense muscles under. He had never seen the big warrior-like sounding so hostile.

Something was off with Josh's attitude, but he couldn't see what. What Rob knew, instinctively, is that the big man would not tell him anything.

He walked through the swinging doors of the kitchen.

"Well, while you're buying things, I'll clean out the mess," he said.

Henry followed then young man inside.

"I'll help you," the cook said. "Then I'll take the rest of the day off."

26 - CLEAN UP

HENRY AND ROB WORKED EFFICIENTLY. They managed to put most of the shards of glass in garbage bags, the weight of the broken glass forcing them to use more bags, so the plastic would not get ripped.

While the cook unscrewed the damaged shelves, Rob passed the mop around the bar area, to soak up the water from the melted ice cubes and soggy napkins, but also to catch out the tinier glass fragments laying on the wooden floor.

He had cleaned out broken wares before in the seedy bar. Most tourist went by in flip-flops, and getting shards embedded in their toes would not figure on their agenda. He made sure his mopping was thorough, all the time trying to make sense of this random act of vandalism.

He gave a light push forward with the mop to dislodge a mound of napkins. One ice cube, no longer a cube with the corners melted off, rolled away. Rob's eyes followed the little ball, its kinetic energy sufficient to get it across the whole terrace floor, then off the stairs.

Such a tiny ball, that had been a perfect one-inch sided cube...

Rob's hands clenched on the handle. The breath caught in his throat.

The ice cubes, half-melted when he had stepped on the terrace, a half-hour before.

Henry had said the vandals had come late in the night, in the early hours when the pier would be deserted, drunk from "whatever shit they had taken", and loosen off their frustrations by breaking anything that was accessible.

But.

Rob picked up another ball of ice. The cold sphere still had a quarter-inch diameter. When he had happened on the scene, the ice cubes were still mostly *cubes* with rounded edges.

The young man had worked at the seedy bar long enough to be able to guess at the time required for a ice cube to melt completely at room temperature.

Ice melted at different rates in air or water. In water, the cubes dissolved fast, because the more tightly packed molecules in the liquid allowed more contact with the ice. But in air, there were contact with the gaseous molecules, so less heat transfer. And at the early summer morning temperature, the ice taken from the ice machine would have taken longer. At around 18 C, the ice cube would take around two hours to melt completely.

And the cubes had had the leisure to become spheres. And the half-inch size of those spheres told him that the vandalism had occurred barely *one hour and a half ago*. So the thugs had stepped on this terrace, maybe *minutes* before Rob arrived. He shivered, from after-trauma.

If he had happened on them, early morning, alone...

He shook of those thoughts and skipped the steps to the promenade. His breath was ragged as he surveyed the facades of the craft shop, the coffee, the vanilla-white ice cream shack, its serving window closed.

None of the other shops had sustained damage. If *Rob* had been on a rampage bend, he would have plundered the ice cream shop first, it being the farthest from the Ocean avenue.

The the young man thought about it, the more he felt the Kon Tikki had been targeted.

Then, he remembered Josh's behavior when he though Rob wasn't looking, his edginess about the fire, the way he was looking at the yellow paper the other day...

My other place was torched to the ground.

He looked again at the white ice cream shack. The two anglers might have seen the vandals, or heard the sound of breaking glass… If Josh had called the cops, they might retrace the guys, get their testimony. Rob had not paid much attention to them, except to notice how fit those tourists were, younger than the old men sitting there sometimes. Maybe they had been war veterans in search of a quiet spot.

Suddenly, Rob the comment of "general Kathleen", about how the fishes population were dwindling and nobody was fishing from the pier anymore, bubbled up in his mind.

They had walked to the end of the pier and plopped their canes there, using the angling as a cover, before doing their deed. Then they had taken their things and gone back to the parking.

The only flaw in their plan was that Rob had decided to rise very early to try his solution, allowing himself enough time to try out his solution.

But now, a vastly more complicated problem was looming over the horizon like a large thundercloud. What had Josh brought from NY, besides his incredible self?

27 - TARGET

Josh was at the counter of the Tool Barn, paying for two cartons of plastic glasses and other necessities, when he spotted his new server through the front window. Rob was making small talk with one of the two pro-life zealots picketing the health center. He had a gaudy plastic bag in one hand.

He wondered if the redhead had taken a taxi to get here from the pier.

When he came out, with two extra-sized yellow plastic bags, Rob saluted one of the women, visibly pregnant, and hurried to his side.

"What are you doing here? I told you to get the day off."

"Henry gave me a ride here."

Then, Rob's thin fingers closed around his wrist. He leaned over, his red curls brushing by his ear.

"Boss, we need to talk," he said in a low voice.

The unexpected intimate contact made Josh reel with of joy, then anguish. Fear and conditioned air send cold shivers through his spine, despite his long-sleeved hoodie.

In reflex, he scanned the mall's plaza for any sign of danger. There was the usual crowd under the icicle ceiling weeping sappy tunes, the pro-life ladies, the early-morning coffee place patronized by the municipal workers. Rafe's "extended family" would have stuck out like dark, sore spots among the summer-clad tourists.

"There nothing to talk about," he said, hating the defensive tone in his voice.

Suddenly, he felt an urge to get out of this too-open place with the icicles ceiling. He walked faster, the elf still latched to his arm.

"Yes there is," Rob said, his eyes two ice marbles. "It was not a random act, it was a target—"

Josh talked over him.

"*Not here!*"

He amended his tone.

"Please, don't talk here."

They passed the glass doors, leaving the weeping music and the conditioned air behind. The temperature had picked up, but Josh kept his hoodie.

Rob stuck with him, until they were out of the parking, on Main street. There were three kilometers to walk to get back to Ocean street.

He felt marginally better as they put more distance from the mall. He turned once, expecting a dark limousine to shadow their steps, but nothing but a lime green jeep with frats boys and a Blue Ford 150 turned out.

Josh tried to put his thoughts in order. He had been a fool to hire the elf, whose tantalizing hips swayed, brushing his bags. He would have to play it by ear, if he wanted to save both of them.

28 - CONFESSION

THE ASPHALT around the abandoned factory was cracked like a crocodile skin, with bushes erupting here and there. Insects screeched from the clumps of wild grass stems reaching as high as them. Rob remembered the games the band of children had played there in the weekend, when the asphalt was whole and the factory empty.

"If you're looking for a private space around here, you won't find it," Rob had said. "However, I know a spot where I played as a kid."

Josh had relented. It had taken the two men twenty minutes to get there, Josh casting anxious glances at each car passing by them. *He's really upset*, Rob thought.

He guided Josh to the side of the two-story building. They crossed a small recess near the emergency staircase, that had been a break place for the smokers, where one picnic table was slowly rotting away. The door had had a mesh across its window. Some teenagers had smashed the glass, but the mesh grid was holding fast.

"The table there?" Josh asked, slowing down.

"No. There's a better place," he said.

Josh pushed his yellow bags under the table. Rob added his own small bag, taking only a water bottle, leaving the plastic-wrapped sandwiches from the Tikki kitchen for later. He had made two egg sandwiches, fairly certain Josh had not eaten before before leaving Henry and him to the cleaning.

He led his gentle giant to a low shed that prolonged the building, its steel back door closed by chains. The shed was completely hidden from the road by the mass of the factory. It had once held the industrial-sized refrigerating unit. The hum of the fridge electrical motor had been a constant background noise behind the sounds of their children contests.

He found with relish that the frost fence behind was ripped open. The rip was wide enough to let them slip into another world, of leafy trees and rustling bushes, and birds calling. A squirrel squeaked as they passed by it. In the forest shade, the temperature was cool temperature was comfortable, not even stuffy.

"Here," Rob said.

It was a maple, the base of the trunk running low on the ground before shooting up. It made for a bench, a bench that Rob knew well from his teenage years, full of tires and shy, tentative kisses with girls who found him cute, and later, from boys who found him to their taste.

Josh sat besides him, straight-backed, his dark eyes darting around as if he expected at any moment an angry bear to burst from the thickets. There hadn't been a bear sighting in a long time, even if the *possibility* of a bear was an enticing danger adding spice to kissing girls and boys...

Rob smiled to himself. If any brown bear happened upon them, the beast would take one look at the smoldering hunk sitting besides him, and flee as fast as it could on its squat paws.

Not the case for Rob: the proximity of the big man played with his senses. Josh smelled of soap and salty sweat. He was like a sullen teen, full of bottled up anger, wary of any adult trying to tame him. Rob was itching to touch him, but he refrained from edging too close, lest all that contained energy flared.

The sole dangerous animals in the woods would be the feral dogs hunting in packs, but those also gave the humans a wide berth. The largest beasts around them were a couple of red chipmunks too embroiled in their chattering pursuits to spare any attention to the two humans sitting motionless.

The rumor of the road, filtered through the trees, made for a low white noise. Rob could imagined themselves sitting on deserted island, or a remote mountain, untouched by the many nuisances of the civilized world. The whispering of leaves, the chirping of a dozen different birds filled the silence, occasionally broken by a series of high-pitched squeals from one of the chipmunks.

Gradually, the tension leaked from Josh's massive body, his wide shoulders slumping forward, his breaths lengthening. When Rob judged that enough time had passed, he added his voice to the wildlife's concert.

"So, what is going on with the Tikki?"

For a few chirps and tweeps, Rob thought he would not get an answer. Then Josh shifted, pulling one knee up, resting his chin on it.

"Before telling you that," he said, "I must go back to my first restaurant. The Lucky Traveler"

"The one that was burned?"

"Yeah. That one."

29 - THE LUCKY TRAVELER

JOSH PAUSED. He felt Rob's attentive eyes locked on him.

Opening himself entailed a risk. Was he ready to take that step? He rolled back his sleeves, exposing the marvelous dragon designs he had had made in New-York while he worked up the restaurant ladder from cook to chef, hidden from everyone under his white uniforms.

Only here had he dared showing them in public. His grandfather would have been proud of the Maori black and blue ink design. The tattoo artist had been a Navajo man who was well-read in many cultures. He only regretted having sacrificed his wealth of hair when he quit the big city. For nothing, it seems, since the family had retraced him here. *Grandpa would never recognize me.*

He stared at the twisted oak tree standing a dozen of paces from him. The bark had been seared by a thunderbolt. Rolls of light-toned fresh bark were closing over the blackened wound. The tree was sending strong limbs up, ending in thousands of green leaves. The complete healing would take years, but the hollow would remained for the rest of the tree's life. He felt like this tree, with a hollow inside.

If he opened a door, he had to open it all the way, and expose the hollow at his center. He had to trust the red-haired elf.

"I was the co-owner of that restaurant," he said. "I had an associate in that venture, who provided the funds to open my place. It was a dream come true."

He told his story, his voice low. How Rafe had recruited him, how they had drafted ambitious plans, how Rafe had come with the investment, how the place had been a resounding success. How his parents had been proud of their son…

"But why would the mob torch it?" Rob asked.

"On the surface, money was flowing, the restaurant was getting even. Under the surface, it seemed my… my associate had been fudging the accounts, gambling away the profits, getting into debts. Getting new loans to pay off the old debts."

He paused, while the familiar ache of betrayal roiled in his stomach. Why hadn't Rafe told him of his money problems? Didn't he trust Josh? But what could the young chef have done to avert the family's anger? He only knew a few of them. And he hadn't nay inkling of the threat, until it was too late.

The ball of guilt bounced back and forth in his head, until a low, velvet-soft voice still it.

"So, the fire," Rob said, to prod the conversation onward.

"The Lucky traveler had it coming, but I was too busy to notice the signs," he said, to the scarred tree. "The mob enforcers sent an arsonist."

He sighed.

"After the insurance paid for the damages, I sold the ruins to some businessmen (and don't ask me if they were part of the mob, 'cause I didn't want to know) and left the Big Apple for good."

"Your associate didn't buy it back?"

Josh's hands on his knee tensed.

"The cops found his body in the ruins."

Rob let out an audible gasp.

"Did they find his murderer?"

"No, but it bore the hallmarks of a mob execution. A shot through the head."

The young elf almost sprang from the bark, passing one hand over his curly hair.

"Oh, shit man!" He said, turning abruptly to face him, his sky blue eyes bristling. "Now I see why you were jumping at shadows!"

Josh's voice got heavier.

"I wished I had been there," he said. "But I was away, on an errand out of town."

Josh recalled their last conversation in the posh apartment with a view on the river.

That money you took...

You worry too much. The Family knows me. They know I always pay back my debts, and I will. I have many more lines in the water, and I will soon reel in one big fish. And then, I'll take you for a trip around the world.

He had wanted to protest, but the silver fox had him well in hands, materially and psychologically.

But, the Giordanos will want to know where their money went!

Nimble hands had played his ribs and abs like a brown piano, then plunged deeper.

They will pardon me once they see how well their funds will have fructified. Now, let's see if I can make you veer off those dark thoughts…

And Rafe had sent the younger man in a spiral of frenzy, stretching him to his limits like an elastic band, until every thought crumbled, until his overworked body gave in to blessed sleep.

When he had awaken, hours later, Rafe had left.

Rob paced to evacuate the load of indignation, horror, and dismay that boiled inside him. Journals and TV stations often exposed protection rackets, but you rarely got to see the impact on the business owner.

His foot hit the base of the twisted thunder-struck tree that had been whole, all those years ago. The sharp pain in his toes echoed in his ankle, his leg and spine. Of course, the tree didn't respond in kind (*that* tree had only been kindness to the young boy he once was), but the jerk move had loosened some of the built-in tension.

He sat down.

The man besides him had fallen silent like a boulder. Rob could sense the waves of guilt underlying the words when Josh had mentioned the errand. The reason why he had not been there when the fire occurred.

The silence stretched for a dozen breaths, filled with the normal forest noises and faraway road noises. The man who had pulled him from the closet had been rattled hard.

His associate, and friend, dead. Maybe, more than a friend. Rob suddenly itched to ask: *Did you love him?* But he refrained. That was a too brutal, in-your-face, inquisition-like question that would shake the big man.

"That guy, Rafe," Rob asked, taming his curiosity under a soft voice. "Were you, er, you know, together?"

A nod forward of the big head, the dragon tails darkened.

Psychology 101, Rob thought. Working side by side in business, day after day, often led collaborators in bed together. That was how Rob's parents had met, after all.

"What kind of man was he?" he asked.

Josh shifted to a more comfortable position, pulling up his other knee.

"Rafes... Rafe was a cool cat," he said. "Older, but very handsome. He loved good food, fine wine, classical music. He had a wide culture, an interest in history, too. He could talk hours about the ancient Greeks, or about his latest shipment of Tuscany wines. He always liked to get me new clothes."

Rob arched a red eyebrow, looking at the ugly hoodie.

"Like this?" he said.

But his friend put one brown hand over the worn fabric.

"No, more fashionable threads. But he knew I liked comfy sweaters. He got me this one, said there was a magic charm sewn inside."

Magic charm? Oh, brother! Rob thought. But he said nothing. Talking about his lost love was good for his friend. Already, Josh's voice had lost its dark edge as he reminisced.

"He was a charmer. My folks absolutely loved him. Rafe was the perfect gentleman, and funny to be with, never a care in the world. When he told me he had pay back the restaurant loan in full, I believed him, and went on my buying trip in the south."

The well of sorrow was pushing up under those last words. *He must be living everyday with the guilt,* Rob thought.

"You said he gambled?"

"He was risk taker. It was, well, a trait my younger self admired in him. Easier to list the casinos he didn't visit than the ones he did. High-end places, of course. Always planning, always one step ahead, full of mischief with his family…"

Rob guessed what "family" meant. Unbidden, the magazine cover pic rose, with the cool dead dude on it. He hadn't looked up the name, but *my, that smile!*

GENTLY PRODDED by the younger man, Josh talked about the loans and risky gambles his dashing associate had explained to him. Rob seemed to follow along, even when Josh mentioned about pyramids and short-term trade, and kite loans.

"A kite loan?" Rob asked, one eyebrow arched.

"Well, it's kind of like a payback check that is paid to another account, while that same account sends another check's at the first one, the same time, er…

Josh let the sentence die unfinished, as his mind tried the recapture his dead lover's explanations. When he had asked the question, Rafe's answer had been so crystal-clear… He felt ashamed of himself, of being so illiterate financially. No wonder Rafe had often seen him as a child.

"Well, that's about that," Josh concluded.

Despite his lame answer, Rob perked up.

"Oh! I get it. The term, at the time, was a *kite-check*. It's a check drawn against uncollected funds in an account, sent and cashed in another account, that emits a second check to a third account. That scheme only works when banks do not talk to each other fast enough."

Josh blinked. Had he dreamed, or had his new server spouted banking terms as it it were chocolate?

"I know how to run a restaurant, but the rest of the stuff eludes me."

"Tell me, what kind of business arrangement did you and Rafe have for the restaurant?" Rob asked. "Were you a LLC, or a C-Corp? Or a LP, a limited partnership?"

Those L- and C- letters flew by Josh's mind like gulls flapping away. He was amazed someone could even spout the words without getting confused.

"I, I have no idea," he said. "Rafe was the one doing the papers."

Rob let out a sigh.

"This is important, 'cause the structure of business partnership means different things for you. For instance, if you are in a LP, a limited partnership, it means one of the partners will be personally liable for business debt. In a LLC, a limited liability company, your assets will be protected if the other partner goes in debts.

"So I would be liable for Rafe's debts?"

"Yes, and if you were in a informal partnership, both of you could be liable."

"I don't know."

Josh didn't dare look at his elf.

"You seem fluent in those matters," he said.

"Well, yeah, I studied business economics before getting expelled from college."

The declaration almost made Josh leap from the bench.

"You were expelled?" he said, unable to keep the indignation from his voice.

A lopsided smile stretched the elf's lips.

"I guess I was less fluent in matters of the heart."

Rob cast a gaze sideways, at the thunderstruck tree. A sunray from the canopy hit the flaming curls of hair tumbling over the young elf's brow. Josh's heart throbbed with excitement, at discovering a new talent. Not only was he well-read, but also savvy in financial matters…

Liar, liar, liar!

Gulls were not among the usual forest dwellers, but flocks of them passed over the trees. No, Josh was excited, enthralled by the proximity of the younger man. *As for matters of the heart, I can help with that, at least*, he thought.

Then he pushed that foul desire away. *He is my employee, now! I can't take advantage of him.*

"With that insurance money, why didn't you open a new restaurant in NY?" Rob asked.

Josh's strong fingers were almost crushing the bark, as he shook his head. He had used the fire insurance money, and the lump sum from the sale of the lot to get out. The fire, and the murder, had left him too heart-broken to think.

"No. I was the public face of the place. That fire had sullied my reputation as a *chef*. Prospective clients would associate me with *mobsters*."

Josh bit in the *mobster* word like a piece of hardened meat. *No more high-end cooking*, he thought. The muscles of his jaw grew tense, with the lines around his downturned lips that Rafe used to tease with a manicured finger.

"I had to get away from there, off to a new start. Safe Harbor looked good to me. And safe."

Rob had edged close to him. He did not resist when deft fingers began massaging his rock-hard neck.

"Well, safe until this morning," he added.

He had never shared his story before, not even his parents (whom he wrote regularly, never leaving a return address nor an email trace). He rose his eyes to the leaves whispering over him. The relief and a deep lassitude washed over him.

Under the canopy, the elf's hands kneaded his deltoids. Rob's thin fingers were surprisingly strong, as they dug into his shoulders, then progressed lower, sending a renewed excitement along his spine. Josh was happy, but at the same time, aware of the danger he placed on the younger man's head.

"Don't," he said.

He could break the frail elf in two if he didn't pay attention. Josh grabbed his employee's shoulders, swiveling his light body over his lap.

Strategic error: now he was facing that impish smile, the blue pair of eyes, the rose lips, half parted. And the buttocks, right on target. Oh, Lord… He couldn't hide his mounting reaction to the younger man.

"We can't," he said, his breath getting ragged. "They'll come after you if…"

Before he could finish, Rob's arms pulled his head down, then his lips, light as petals, closing over his own.

The kiss was unexpected, and fierce. Josh felt a jolt of electricity coursing through his body, a flowering sensation that felt so incredibly *right*, a feeling he hadn't felt since, since…

Rafe.

Rafe who had died because of him. He made a last effort to disengage himself from the embrace.

"You know what happened," he said. "I can't drag you in this…,"

But words failed him when two bright, blue eyes teared down his layers of defiance.

"Hey, big boy," Rob said. "It's too late, now. Let me help you."

The young elf pulled Josh's black tee over his head, each part of the gesture alternating with kisses. Josh didn't remember rolling off the tree and lying down, but he heard the crackle of fallen leaves under his bare skin, he breathed the earthy smells rising from the soft humus, the tickling of his nose by the sun-warmed red hair, the sensation of the sun-spotted back moving under his hands, and the sweetness of the rest of the thin body exploded in his mind, along with their laughter.

30 - CLOSE ENCOUNTER

When Rob opened his eyes, later, he knew what happiness felt. For a minute, he let the calls of the birds and the rustling of the wind fill his mind.

He had conquered his own fear, and the fears of his warrior. He rose on one elbow, wary of the hidden roots running under the dried up leaves near the cracked tree. They had rolled to and fro, leaves crackling like a bonfire under their bare backs. He looked at the powerful body of the man sleeping besides him, his lips parted on too-white teeth. Rob resisted the urge to trace the beardless jaw, to explore again those white pearls inside the wide mouth.

Exhaustion, sheer mental and nervous exhaustion, had taken its toll, and he didn't want to wake his friend.

Friend for now, even if the big man evoked a host of warring emotions inside him. Desire, fear, wariness, attachment.

Yeah, he could get used to it…, no, he *was* quite attached to the hunk.

But Rob had been burnt before, scorched like that tree looming over their tangled bodies. He was not tempted to take the plunge into a long lasting commitment. For now, the physical interlude had melted the ice between them.

Now that he had a better grasp of Josh's problems. Rob resolved to help him find a solution to counter the threat. His stomach groaned, loud enough to wake his neighbor.

Rob quickly retrieved his clothes and shoes, and pulled them on, after using the water from his bottle to clean the last traces of their shared pleasure.

He had a hunger for a more satisfying food, recalling the sandwiches hidden under the old table. He would surprise his warrior with a kiss and a snack.

He clambered down the rush to the rip in the fence, checking the traffic sounds. Then he ran around the refrigerating shack, his steps echoing on the pebbles there. He slowed down to follow the aisle leading to the recess. He stopped by the emergency ladder, casting a circular sweep of the picnic table and the yellow bags lying over. The rumble of motor down Main avenue bounced on the three high walls of the recess.

He advanced inside the recess, to retrieve the food carton, then paused. Had not Josh pushed the bags *under* that table? From the corner of his eye, he spied a flash of lime green among the rushes winked at him.

A parked car.

Rob tensed in alarm as a light crackling of plastic sounded behind him, like someone zipping up a sandwich bag. Just as he realized he was not alone, strong arms grabbed him.

In an instant, a burst of *fight or flight* adrenaline reaction rushed through his body. He opened his mouth to warn Josh. His shout was muffled by a thick pad of gauze pressed on his face, almost broking his nose in the process. The centered pain shot his vision in tones of red.

He drew breath to call again, inhaling a powerful alcohol-like stench that made his eyes water.

Rob raised his hands to push at the gag, but fingers hard as an iron vise clamped around his right wrist, and pulled it away. The guy held Rob against his toned chest as if he was no more than a child.

Nevertheless, Rob fought his assailant with all his might, as he had fought others at the college gym, twisting his shoulders, the back of his shoes hitting the man's shins, sucking in more corrupted air through the gauze.

His left hand grabbed at a light cotton shirt. He clutched at the fabric, but he was getting heavy-headed, his thoughts wandering away, like in a wild party with too much booze, or a lack of insulin. Voices danced around him, not Josh's, another guy, plural guys, now he was getting more dizzy and disoriented, his vision clouding over.

Rob tried to call out, but his throat closed around a muffled groan. As his knees melted under him, everything fading away, he heard a low, rasping voice with a Bronx accent.

"Hey, handsome, we just *wanna* talk with your buddy."

31 - THE FIXER

JOSH WAS FLOATING on an ocean of delight, hearing soft waves crashing against the sand, like so long ago, when his grandpa took him sailing. his temples. When he opened his eyes on the canopy, he could hear the birds chattering louder. He stretched, a long, feline stretch wondering how many months it had been since he had slept so soundly. It had been more than a year since the last time with...

He rolled over himself, in a careful move, to avoid crushing his love.

Yes, he had said it in his head, the word that he had professed to never use for another man.

Then his body had completed the turn, his questing hand finding only the dried leaves where Rob had lain.

Josh rose himself on his elbows, taking in the sun dappled ground, the curved trunk, the empty place next to him.

He was alone.

Fear shot through him like a dark, cold wave of conflicted emotions. The morning's discovery, his quest to save the Tikki, Rob's following him, his confession, and this delightful interlude… Where had Rob gone? Had he left him?

Uncertainty made his hands tremble as he pulled on his clothes, as he fumbled to knot the flat laces of his running shoes. He looked around, and a deep breath to calm himself.

Maybe his dear little elf had had to relieve himself. That was it. But Rob wouldn't have to go that far for it.

He rose. And waited some more, trying to distract himself with the bird songs. The afternoon was advanced.

No Rob coming out from a thicket, readjusting his pants.

Nothing to do but going back to the ominous factory. He could see the faint outline of the building through the trees.

Josh passed through the rip. He rounded the corner of the shack. No one there. As he followed the aisle to the recess with the table, he saw something flashing. Something green, among the clumps of wild weeds.

A car.

Josh didn't remember having seen it when Rob had taken him to the back. And he had been on his guards when they had crossed the vast expanse. He had seen that green car before.

His heartbeat shot to unhealthy high rate. It could be only tourists. But now his instincts had kicked in as he approached the recess.

When he was about to pass the steel ladder, a two loud bass measures of Sold-Out Boys exploded in the small recess, bouncing around, creating multiple echoes. Despite his cautions, he jumped almost a mile high at the nerve-pinching barbarous music.

Someone was here, someone without a care about discretion.

He bounced inside. He took it all at once, the table, the body sprawled upon – Rob, unmoving – the bags over the table, opened, their content (the paper cups, napkins and other plastic bags) spread over the benches, the napkins squares opened like white doves.

He rushed to Rob, almost reliving the very first time he had laid eyes on the young elf, faint from lack of insulin. But it was not dinner time yet, so he slowed down, suddenly wary. Even if he had felt weak, Rob would not have sprawled himself like an opened oyster. He gripped the shoulders and shook, gently.

"Hey, hey," he called.

But his elf didn't respond, his jaw slack. That's when Josh noticed the reddish burn on the patrician nose, and the half-opened mouth. As Josh leaned closer, he got a whiff of a thick smell, like the methanol disinfectant he used on some rusted utensils.

Josh put his ear against the parted lips, and was relieved to feel a shallow breeze coming out. His elf wasn't dead, but out cold.

"Hey," another voice called, from high.

Josh turned.

His knees went weak as he recognized the Fixer, his lean body wedged in the steps of the ladder, one full body height over him. He was wearing a crisp white shirt and Men-In-Black dark suit.

"If it isn't my best pal's wild boy," he said, with his affected Bronx accent.

Before Josh could lift Rob's limp frame off the table and flee, two men sprouted from the clumps of yellowing weeds covering the parking. They were similarly garbed like idle tourists, the Bermudas and flowery shirts, and caps, and the thick-soled leather sandals.

The sole difference was the desert-colored semi automatic rifles they held pointed in his direction. He was instantly aware of the focused heat of two laser targeting beads on his black Tee-shirt.

32 - HARD TRUTHS

RAFE'S BEST "PAL" had had that kind of ovoid-shaped head that he had tried to compensate by ruffling up his wavy black hair. Under the mass of hair --most certainly colored because the man was about Rafe's age--, his brow was narrow, creased with frown lines. In contrast, the corners of his mouth were eternally lifted up in a mocked smile.

Josh had met Jimmy Fixi often at the Lucky Traveler best booth, sprawled over his part of the well padded seats, tasting the meals, critiquing the young chef 's *savoir faire*.

In those occasions, Rafe had always exhibited a calm demeanor, using his dazzling smile as a beacon to drew the rest of the Giordano family's attention to him instead, leaving the Fixer to stew in his juice. Josh knew the family's attitude about sexual orientation, their view being traditional, heteronormative. Rafe had always kept their relationship a secret, putting Josh' apartment lease under another name.

At the time, Josh had nursed a petty resentment, seeing the lease signing as another proof Raphael Giordano didn't consider him as an adult. But now, with the guns trained on him, the red beads sauntering on his chest, his former lover's action took another meaning.

The silver fox had done his best to protect Josh from the onslaught that he knew was coming. Hence the names on the business papers, Josh's name appearing as co-owner, along with the thirty or so employees and waiters of the (un-)*Lucky Traveler*.

Now Josh felt quite unlucky as the man that Rafe had called The Fixer descended the steel stairway, his steps echoing in the enclosure. He was wearing an coal-gray Armani suit similar to the one Rafe had favored.

He turned to check on Rob, but the young man was still flat on his back. His skin had a pale gray tinge that made Josh worry.

"What did you do to him?" he asked.

A floppy smile etched the thin man's lips. He raised one long-fingered, manicured hand. The two red beads left his chest.

"I wanted to have a lil chat, Wild Boy. No witness."

Then, the Fixer advanced near the table. Two long fingers pressed the side of the young man's slender neck.

"Pulse steady. Your cutie is just sleeping his stress away."

He picked up a transparent sandwich bag from the ground, with what Josh made up as a thick napkin inside. The fixer pressed the bag in one hand. A whiff of a strong alcohol-like fume made his eyes water.

"Chloroform, from the family's lab. Be content that I have come prepared, because otherwise…"

The slender fingers spread like spider legs around the pale neck.

"No!" Josh cried out.

"Oh, so you really care for him? I'm surprised."

The hand left the neck.

"For *now*, your cutie's living," he said.

"You followed us."

"Intelligent boy. Yes, we tailed you from the mall. And we had to wait while you made those disgusting noises in the forest."

The two light-clothed goons accompanying Fix chuckled. One spat a few yellow gobs of mush from the egg-sandwich he had been wolfing down. The egg sandwich Rob had made this morning. Josh prayed his darker skin did not betray his own embarrassment, but his face was heating up like a furnace.

"Sit," the Fixer said.

Josh obeyed, under the four eyes of the goons. He straddle the wooden bench, close to Rob's upturned head, keeping one leg out.

"So, you see, wild boy, cutting your hair and disappearing in the boondocks had been a good move."

Josh blinked.

"How did you find me?"

Fingers pinched his chin. The touch had an unexpected element of warmth in it, contrasting with the cold demeanor of the Fixer.

"We were trying to retrace your moves, wild boy, for two years. Your folks knew squat about your current location. They were nice enough to show me the postcards, but that got me nowhere. Finally we got a break when your stupid mayor published the pics of your new place on the net. Technology did the rest. You know, face recognition and all."

Josh had changed his appearance to escape the family's notice. *Everything's fine*, Rafe had said on the phone, that last evening, a thousand kilometers away. *Just enjoy yourself while I'm going fishing.*

The next day the Lucky Traveler had burnt.

Josh looked up at the man who had eaten so often at the restaurant, the obvious question burning his eyes. *Why?*

The hand dropped.

"So you thought you would be able to fool the family, wild boy?" the Fixer said, walking to and fro.

"Fool the family? I don't know what you're talking ab—"

Jimmy Fix's palm struck his cheek so fast Josh had no time to recoil. One second, the dark-haired man was casually walking past him, the next, his hand had shot out. The slap sounded loud in the enclosed space.

"Playing the innocent, now, are you? When you and Rafe stole a fricking *ninety million* dollars, and hid it so well nobody could retrace it."

Josh was flabbergasted. The initial investment required to renovate the space, hire the personnel and start the restaurant had totaled a fair four hundred thousands, not counting Rafe's own non-negligible reserves. The success of the *Lucky Traveler* as a high-end dining place had paid back that investment.

"*N-ninety* million?" he said, incredulous. "Impossible!"

"Yep," the Fixer said, his own weaselly face twisted in an half smile. "And the family has given me with the daunting task of finding where their monies went."

A surge of anger washed over Josh. He grabbed the lapels of the dark suit, baring his teeth.

"You should have asked Rafe, *before gunning him down!*"

Josh barely had time to see the Fixer moving before an impact on his solar plexus cut his breath.

He fell from the bench, trying to breathe, not succeeding, while his brain managed subsequent alarm signals coming from his stomach, his arms, his back… This was no bar brawl. Despite his being stronger than the three men present, not counting the guns, Josh couldn't retaliate without getting his elf in more danger.

His elf… Josh should never had let the flame-haired, anime-eyed man into his life. He should not have listened to his burning desire and hire Rob.

He let out a groan when one pointed shoe connected with his soft genitals. Then his lower ribcage. He heard a moist crack, then more pain as a floating rib must have fractured. A red fog clouded his vision, as he was still trying to reap some oxygen from the air.

Then, somehow, as he was coaxing more volume into his lungs, the rain of blows abated.

Four hands grabbed him and propped him against the emergency ladder. Thin metal wires bit his wrists as his hands were bound to the railing, then his ankles to the lower bars, the wire scissoring the skin over his shin bone. He became dimly aware his tee shirt had been removed.

Presently, the man known as the Fixer balled the dark cloth in one hand. Then he cast the ball of cloth on the table, next to Rob's shoes.

"You're insulting me, wild boy."

The goons drew closer, the one with the flowery Bermuda shorts cracking his joints for another fist fest. Josh expected his life to end, here and now.

"Rafe was a good pal-o-mine," Jimmy said, his voice showing an unexpected emotion. "I didn't kill him."

The Fixer's lean face hovered so close that Josh could almost talk to the mole gracing the left cheekbone.

"Make no mistake," he said. "If the Giordano's Don

had ordered me to do so, I would had offed my pal. Because I'm loyal to the family."

He paused, his dark eyes gazing at the bricks behind Josh.

"But he didn't give the order to kill his favorite nephew, that old bleeding heart! And none of the family's other hitmen had received it."

"But who killed Rafe, if not you?"

"That's a good question, but Rafe's burnt crisp wasn't very talkative."

Thanks for the mental image, Josh thought.

He had never seen his lover's charred body. When he had hurried back to NY, the Giordano family had already swooped in. Prodded by their terrible grief, Josh had imagined. *Covering the shame,* he understood now.

Josh had not dared attending the funerals, because of the TV crews there. Raphael had been a darling of the public, the arts patrons. There was a rumor that the Splendid Siblings had attended the funeral mass, but Josh knew the young artists had already gone their separate ways.

Even the Giordano's Don had attended the mass in his wheelchair, his cadre of faithful retinue deviating the journalists' attempt at interview. One rare close up from the TV crew captured the glittering tears on his hard, wrinkled face.

"He was loved," Josh said, almost for himself.

A lopsided grin changed the Fixer's traits. He approached his snarling face inches from Josh's.

"Oh, wild boy, so well-loved, was he, our Rafe, because he had *two other cute boys* set up in their own lush apartments, just like yours!"

Just like yours. The words impacted Josh's mind like

Thor's hammer. He was not aware of his shattered breath until the man emitted an ugly laugh.

"I see this come as news to you, eh?"

Josh's tongue felt like a lump of lead.

"You're lying!" he said, his voice shaky.

But no gull passed over them, calling *Liar, liar*.

33 - BETRAYAL

Josh, lovesick, had kept a count in his mind of all the nights he lied alone between the satin sheets of the King bed, looking at the waters of the Hudson, wondering where his silver fox was, if he was safe.

Rafe had told him in covert terms about his business meetings abroad and important errands to do, and of the need to keep his own cover, at his lush Queens mansion. Rafe's unmarried, dilapidated lifestyle annoyed his family; but if they learned of his queer nature, the consequences could be dire.

And now, all those absences, those meetings had another explanation. Josh closed his eyes. Had Rafe brought his other flames in his restaurant? Eating under his nose… Secretly laughing at him…

This was a nightmare. Josh had always been loyal.

Even when he had the inklings of a money laundering scheme, seeing Rafe's family and friends always eating "on the house", he hadn't broached the subject. And that last "gamble" his silver fox was alluding about, would have been this theft.

He heard the scrunched gravel as the Fixer walked to Rob's sprawled form.

Josh's inner turmoil rose like mercury in a thermometer. He had never felt so powerless, immobilized, trussed up like a chicken about to get grilled. He bit his lips, afraid any outburst from him would aggravate the Fixer.

Again, manicured fingers traced the delicate jaw, applying just enough pressure to make his elf's head roll on its side, a lock of red hair curling over the ivory brow.

"To make the story short, wild boy, the family's accountant looked into all of Rafe's accounts. With *nada* results. So I need you to tell me about those mil. What was done with it?"

Josh was still trying to come to terms with this deception, when the Fixer talked again.

"I see how you look at him. True love, ooh!" he crooned, to the snickers of his men.

The Fixer's hand flew in a side pocket. A casual gesture, as if to pull a tissue, before Josh glimpsed the flicker of a switchblade. Jimmy Fix's wrist flashed, and a lock of red hair fell drifted down.

"So I don't want to hurt your boy toy here, but if you force me…"

Josh felt panic rising in his throat, mixed with a sour disgust. Jimmy Fix would be the kind of machos to use that expression.

"But the loan have *been repaid*!" he said, pounding over the words. "I never saw those millions you're talking about, not even the paper work. I opened the Kon Tikki here with the money from the fire insurance!"

The Fixer's knife hung over the exposed neck.

"Not good, wild boy. As a joint owner, you sold the ruins at such a lousy price."

At that time, Josh had been only thinking of fleeing.

"We checked the paper trail. Rafe was right, he paid back the *Lucky Traveler*'s debts, along with his own gambling debts, with our family's nest egg. But he didn't stop there."

Jimmy made a siphoning sound

"…your lover *drained* the whole Don's account, leaving only thirteen cents. That had been the last straw. The money had vanished, and we think your sweet Rafe had funneled it in some fiscal paradise."

Josh was out of his depth. A lot of good that paradise account was for a dead man!

"So try to think. There must be something you, and only you, would know."

"What about, the, the other lovers?" Josh asked.

The words twisted his very soul. The secret pride of a being loved by such a dashing, brilliant man, when others had always seen him as brainless hunk, good at nothing except making meals, that pride had sustained him through the eleven-hours days of the Lucky Traveler's kitchen.

The gleaming counters and steam washing machine and the thousand-dollar-worth of updated appliances, destroyed.

"Oh, I shook'em long before I found you, wild boy. But it seems our Rafe told them squat about his fine maneuvers. Which leaves you, wild boy."

Josh tried to remember what Rafe had told him about his accounts. But he came with nothing. He never tried to pry in his lover's finances.

"Rafe, he had a safe, at his own place. The papers might…"

"First place we tried. Do better."

Jimmy Fix flicked his wrist, and the blade arched, too

close to Rob's neck. Another red curl flew, drifting to the packed earth.

"I'm thinking, I'm thinking!" Josh said, as the man stepped towards him.

"Check for company," he said to the goons.

The Bermuda pair went out, sniggering.

A finger traced Josh's abs. Then turned to the pectorals, and back down, in a spiral that Josh suddenly interpreted as a big number "9".

"Think well, wild boy."

Josh scrunched his eyes shut, hard. He had just told Rob about the kite thing. There might have been more schemes Rafe hadn't imparted, like he had never mentioned what he did for a living before they met.

Rafe, so risk-taking, devious. So sure of himself. Of the two of them. He made grand projects, maybe puffs of air.

Someday, I'll take you for two-year a trip around the world, Rafe had said. With his expensive tastes, ninety million might just cover the costs.

Rafe, always planning, always one step ahead… always gambling.

Josh moistened his lips, hoping no damn gull flew over them. He let a slow, silent breath escape his lips. Time to take a gamble of his own.

"I t-think Rafe talked to me, once, about having an offshore account. A secret one."

Fear clutched at his throat, making him talk haltingly. But the slimy fingers on his torso paused.

"Keep talking, wild boy."

"I, I don't remember the number, or password. But I can make enquiries…"

No gull crossed the rectangle of blue sky over the enclosure.

"That is, if you give me some time. I'm pretty sure I can find it."

The Fixer flicked off the blade and pushed the jack-knife in his pocket.

"That my boy," he said, his voice suddenly warm as an doting uncle. "We'll leave your place alone. We'll leave your parents alone, too.

Josh sucked up air, seeing his folks, loving, vulnerable.

"I give you one week to com up with the intel. If the intel proves right, you'll be off the hook. The family will forget your existence."

"But, I can't guarantee the amount will still be there."

Strong fingers framed his chin.

"Then, you will account for what's missing, wild boy."

THE BERMUDA GOON walked toward the car, while the Fixer collapsed the guns inside a wallet. A breath of relief escaped Josh's lips.

A fist struck his jaw, sending stars into his eyes. He had lost sight of the second goon. As he reeled from the pain, a hand pushed a tight roll of cloth inside his mouth.

His protest went inaudible, as his airways were clogged. He tried to push off the gag with his tongue, but the same goon knotted a gaudy-colored scarf around his head, over his mouth.

Then, the crafty Fixer deposited Josh's cell phone at his feet.

"Now, be a good boy and don't go weeping to the police, nor try to find us before D-day," he said, his brown eyes mocking. "Your cutie will wake up and unbind you."

Another smile, as the man's hands snaked down,

cupping his crotch. Josh sensed a wave of nausea rising up. He understood now all the snide comment about his meals, the angry stares.

The Fixer himself had been secretly in love with Rafe.

And Rafe had rejected him. That's how he knew so much about the other lovers stashed away.

"Unless your cutie likes to play with ropes," the Fixer said with a chuckle.

He turned and walked away. Josh tried to cry out, but the rag pressed his tongue down, tickling his uvula, which in turn gave him an urge to sneeze. He felt dizzy from the lack of air, and thirsty.

He made himself breathe slowly, and a few atoms of oxygen got to his lungs, but not enough. The stupid goon had made a smothering gag.

The sound of the green car dwindled away.

The pain on his sides and belly had receded under his lungs' pressing need. He made himself breathing slow, slower, so the folded gag would not clog his airways more that they already did. He thought of the zen masters, able to slow their breath.

His additional mental anguish did not help getting to a zen state.

Rafe, his dear silver fox, had not only gambled away the restaurant's earnings like he had feared, and lied to him about the loans, but he had entertained other lovers in separate apartments. Then, he had gone on his supposedly benign "wager" and stolen an outlandish amount from his own family!

Josh had no idea how he would come by himself with such an amount. The new restaurant had engulfed the money that had landed into Josh's account. He would have to work days and nights, maybe take a second job, for years and years, before coming up with the amount. Or win the lottery.

Oh, how he had believed Rafe's syrupy words of reassurance! The loans that had never existed, the seed money, and more, that had been taken from the *family*'s coffers!

As Josh pondered what he would say to his dear elf, he heard a whisper of clothes from the table.

"Are they gone?" a reedy voice asked.

Josh would have cried out with delight, if for the balled fabric in his mouth.

Rob Sundance was pushing himself off the table. He swiveled his legs over the side, totally awake, no trace of grogginess as his manga-blue eyes surveyed the enclosure.

When he saw Josh, an amused smirk curled his lips.

"You know you're full of crap, big boy?" he said.

34 - SHAME

RELIEF AND SHAME warred inside Josh as the young man fumbled with the gaudy scarf's knot. Eventually, he unloosened the scarf down Josh's throat. Then he extracted the moist ball of fabric from Josh's mouth, the color suspiciously like his missing Tee.

"Rob," he began, before an sudden urge of drawing breath stopped him.

"Don't talk now. That gag was asphyxiating you."

While Josh wheezed and sucked in lungful after grateful lungful of air, the young man bent to unknot the bindings around his legs and wrist, emitting a low whistle.

"The turds bought that no2 aluminum wire at the Tool Barn," he said.

He untwisted the ends, and the wires slackened around Josh. He felt the circulation coming back in his hands. A dozen stars danced in front of his eyes, and he felt dizzy.

"You just breathed too fast, and got an oxygen overdose."

He felt Rob's arms around his waist, as he was led to the bench.

When he had gotten his breath back, the anguish replaced his relief. Rob was standing, looking down at him.

"So *that's* what you didn't told me," he said.

Josh eyes went wide.

"What? What did you hear?"

The image of his elf, spread motionless on the table top, the thug casually flicking his knife, still made his voice quaver.

Rob brushed his fingers through his curls, then worked out a kink in his neck, the audible crack of grinding vertebras grating Josh's nerves.

"Well, I got about everything that Bronx-accented thug said after he slapped you."

35 - THE GENTLE ART OF FAKING

Rob HEARD the trembling in Josh's voice as he protested.

"But, you, you were out cold when I reached you, and didn't budge when this turd was playing with his knife around!"

He stretched himself, arms reaching high, to get the ugly paws off his system. The last minutes had been the worst he had ever lived, not counting the men who jumped him.

"Josh, I've had a lifetime of being the smallest in any class, and being harassed, and beaten upon in bars. Faking has become an art I've perfected."

He sat beside the bigger man, patting lightly his thigh.

"I don't remember the guys jumping me, that's kind of foggy, but I came to my senses when I heard a loud slap. And talks about millions, and then, they were beating on you. I heard it, but couldn't decide what to do, against those walking turds."

Josh turned, the white of his eyes showing.

"They would have taken you out. When the Fixer

pressed the blade against your throat, I though I would die. And you tell me you were *conscious?*"

Rob was still reeling from the delayed reaction, after his class acting. The voice of the Bronx-accented man had betrayed his own jealousy as he extolled with relish the rakish Rafe's exploits. Josh anguish shone through his answers.

When fingers had turned Rob's head on the side, he had looked through his lowered lids, to discover the two Bermuda-wearing goons trussing up his friend on the steel ladder. A thin, well-groomed man, his dark hair done high over his narrow brow, was *touching* Josh, whose scrunched features convened his disgust.

When the Bronx-accented man was not satisfied, he walked back.

"He was blabbing, his bad-movie spiel, when I felt the swish of air, and felt my strand brush my cheek."

He fingered the shorter clipped strands rising over his brow.

"I prefer to choose my own hair cutter," he said, drawing a meager satisfaction of seeing a half smile on his warrior's face.

Then, he asked the question burning his lips.

"So, what will you do?"

Josh did not answer yet. He must have been whipping himself, for his past.

"I don't see what else I can do. I'll close the Kon Tikki, get Henry his four percent, and disappear."

Rob caught him self from swearing a loud *C.A.*!

"What do you mean, you'll disappear?"

"I'll talk to my folks and convince them to move some-where else. Then I'll go else where no one can find me."

"You you would go alone? Why? Don't you have to get this account number?"

Josh strong hands gripped his shoulders.

"You don't understand: I lied about Rafe telling me things about an offshore account! Rafe... he did not tell me anything about those million."

Again, Rob caught the edge of betrayal grating in the big man's voice. And something more. The words fell from his mouth as tiny drops of a harsh remedy.

"Oh. I. see."

His lips trembled as he realized Josh had lied to save *him*.

"I, I appreciate that, big boy," he said.

His throat felt like a ball of wool was stuck inside. He spurred on.

"Thanks for saving my bacon. But look, there's no reason for you to flee alone. If you close the Tikki, I can go hide with you in the Rockies. Or in the Nevada desert. Or even in Canada."

A faint smile curled Josh's lips.

"Hot and cold, are you? But no."

The young man stepped of the walls, scanning the expanse of shrub-invaded parking. The thugs were gone, but he needed to rally his mental forces.

He turned to see Josh picking up his backpack, the sleeves of his gray "charmed" hoodie knotted around his waist. Rob's sandwich bag lay, empty. The goons must have eaten well.

He parted his lips to talk. But Josh raised his palm.

"Look, Rob, it's become too dangerous for you to associate with me. So I'll disappear."

The way Josh was keeping him at arm's length was grating at him. A few days ago, Rob would not have minded the big warrior keeping his emotional distance. He himself had wanted a casual, physical relationship. Like a romp in the woods…

Now the idea of letting Josh disappear left his stomach roiling. He would never see his big hunk again. It was more than he could endure, and *that* told him he had fallen, hard.

36 - TWO IS BETTER THAN ONE

Josh LONG LEGS scissored through the parking, making it hard for the younger man to follow him.

"Eh, big boy! Wait!"

Josh walked on, intent on avoiding the cracks. His fractured rib hurt at each step. He should get checked by the kind arab-looking doctor before leaving Safe Harbor for ever. He had made his decision, but no sense of relief followed it.

Josh felt bad at quitting, especially that he had promised Henry, a recovering alcoholic, to help him through the summer. He would drain his local account to give Henry and Rob a fair severance amount.

His heart was heavy at the idea of lying to his folks, again. For all his faults, Rafe had shown real affection for his parents, even covering the cost of his mom's hearing aid. The rare conversations Josh had had with his mom over a pay phone had not left him with a fear for their safety. But this could change, once the Fixer's gang discover he had lied to them.

He spurred on, each steps sending pebbles sideway.

Thinking forward: buy a new cell phone, call his parents… The shorter steps of Rob fell away.

But as he reach the Main avenue's gravel side, the younger man caught up with him, one hand pulling at the strap of his back pack.

"You can't leave like that!" Rob said, his breath ragged.

The car circulation had picked up, mostly families descending to the pier and the beach. Josh turned on his dear, dear elf.

"What don't you understand? I don't want you to get hurt again!"

"And you, big boy? How will you live, alone?"

The impish face was deadly serious, his eyes downcast.

"I'll change states, and change my name. I'll find work somewhere else."

"And you wont try to find the account for the Bronx guy?"

Josh extended his arms in irritation.

"What do you want me to do, to come up with those mil? Win the lottery?"

Josh was no math genius, but he knew the overall chances of winning the jackpot were astronomically low. He made a pistol with his index.

"Unless I rob a bank?"

The idea was preposterous. Josh would never have the callousness to point a pistol in some innocent cashier's face.

"They are a bunch of hoodlums, as you have seen. Their dirty money is no skin off my nose!"

This time, it was Rob's turn to face him like a flame-haired djinn, his eyes murderous.

"No, maybe it is not your problem, but by quitting now, you'll make it a problem for a whole bunch of other, innocent people. Besides your own folks."

WHAT DO YOU MEAN, INNOCENT PEOPLE?"

Rob had the satisfaction of reading the shocked reaction in Josh's face.

"You think Rafe's family would be more competent to rob a bank?"

"Where are you going with that?"

"That, until now, the mobsters have kept a dim hope to retrieve this stolen money from wherever it is. Now, if they abandon this hope, what will they resort to, to recoup their losses?"

Josh' dark gaze was turned to the long stretch of road remaining to get to the bustling village.

"Er, whatever they did to in the first place to get it?"

"Let me help you with that *whatever*, big boy. To make back this amount, Rafe's nice buddies will ratchet up their activities: raised the prices up the protection rackets, extend their prostitution rings, put some new synthetic drugs on the markets, destroying more lives in the process. And hitch up the phone call frauds to net old folks' money."

"They must have made more that ninety million a year. They should take no time to recoup their loss…"

Josh voice trailed off, as he saw what Rob had known since his NY bar tender days.

"No, big boy, they won't look back. Trust me on that. They will keep this upper level of nastiness because they will get addicted to it. Remember the Star Wars movie?"

"Hum, which one?"

"The one where the dictator, that Palpatine guy, asks very nicely of the assembly to grant him special powers, as an exception."

"Oh. It was the start of the Empire."

"Yeah. And, as many present-day dictators, have, demonstrated…"

Rob's breath was getting ragged, as his enthusiasm was not matched by his condition.

"Slow down, big boy."

His friend complied.

"Sorry."

Rob's lungs were parched. The water bottle lay some-where among the casualties, because Josh had been too hurried to get off this place to care about littering.

He looped his arm through Josh's forearm.

"So the "exceptional" situation soon becomes the norm, and the people under the new dictator groan, forcing more "necessary" measures to be taken. And that's not counting some foreign country giving a gentle nudge with a Coup d'État."

Josh bit his lips, then he chased off his breath in an explosive sigh.

"All right, man! I see it. We do the right thing, even if it is giving back ill-gained money. Because, the alternative would be worse for everyone.

He kicked a gravel that bounded on the asphalt.

"To do so, we must find Rafe's hoard, except that, as I already told you, I lied. I know squat about Rafe's treasure, or even if it exists."

Rob smiled, his elfin, high-cheeked face so full of mischief, that Josh was reminded of Rafe.

"Big boy, the fact *you* don't know squat doesn't mean there is no treasure to find."

Josh pointed the obvious.

"I have only one week to find it. And the family already went with microscopes through Rafe's possessions, after the fire."

Rob had an idea coming up.

"After the fire, eh? You know, big boy, maybe that Fixer guy was right when he told you they didn't kill your Rafe. They don't know squat, either."

"Why?"

"Because, if they'd suspected at that time that Rafe had stolen the money, they would not have offed him *before* he spit the morsel."

They walked under the sluggish heat, Josh silent.

A loud hiss of breaks in their backs had the two of them jumping. Josh tensed, letting the backpack slide down, ready to defend their life. Rob pressed his lips together and looked back.

A blue Ford 150 had crept over the gravel side, its left tires encroaching on the grassy abandoned field. A big, pale-haired arm leaned on the driver's window sill. The driver pushed open the door, letting a tempting hum of conditioner seep out of the cabin.

Rob recognized the tousled head of the hulking fish-erman whom he had seen at the store with the nice, crutch-holding Maeve. The big man was smiling like a blond sun.

"You're rather a long way from your place, Mr. Kon Tikki! Care to jump on my horse?"

Unable to resist the power of this carefree smile, Josh returned it.

38 - REGROUP AND RECOUP

THE HULKING FISHERMAN, Stanley, and Josh talked about (what else?) fish all the way to the harbor. Rob huddled in the back seat, content to let the boys talk. Stanley's good humor was contagious, despite what had happened, Josh seemed to loose some of his gloom by asking questions about the fishing.

Since the first time, Stanley had come back twice to eat at the Kon Tikki. The Nordic-looking hunk had no time to linger, being all invested on his project, taking all hours to refit his boat, sparing no expense to comply to the stringent water safety regulations.

"You wouldn't believe the price of all those CSA certified life jackets," he said as they turned on the familiar Ocean View.

So, when Josh offered him to eat free in reward for his timely help, Stanley did not refuse.

"I've just to get those life jackets settled in the boat," he said, and then I'm good."

Stanley parked in his usual space and got out of the

truck. He opened the back hatch and started unloading the life jackets, all wrapped in life-destroying plastic.

"Man, you've got a bunch, here," Josh said.

"I'll make two trips," the big fisherman said, balancing six packets on his arms.

"Let me give you a hand."

Josh arched himself over the hatch to grab the more remote pile of life jackets. As he hefted the pile, a sharp pain zapped his spine. He dropped the life jackets with a startled groan that had Rob and Stanley turn. He tried to smile, to hide the pain, but it was as if a belt of flame had wrapped itself around his waist.

The pain reawakened the other traces of the mobsters' work on his battered body. He wrapped his arms as if to contain an explosion in his ribcage.

"It's nothing," he said, wincing as he bent, slowly, and retrieved the packets.

He caught Rob's anxious gaze, and shook his head. He didn't want to expose his problems to anyone. A silent tip of the red head told him Rob understood. But his lips formed the words *doctor*.

"I'll help you Stan," Rob said. "Josh had to get the things to the restaurant."

As those things were lighter that the life jackets, Josh was back in his kitchen in a jiffy.

He was disposing the new glasses on the main table when he noticed that Henry was sitting, in a corner.

"Henry? Eh, weren't you supposed to take the day off? Seeing some friends?"

The cook shook his gray head.

"Didn't feel like it," he said. "I guess work's my best therapy."

Josh knew the older man wrestled his own demons, but he elected not to press it.

~

It took Rob one half-hour to transfer the life jackets in Stan's blue boat then get back to the restaurant. By then, the adrenaline chased away, he felt all his recent bruises clamoring, as he washed his hands.

When he got back, at the Tikki, Josh and Henry were putting the place in a semblance of order. Josh felt his ribs though the apron he wore.

And Rob *had* heard the crack under the mobster's blows.

As they got the supper menu under way, their boss showed restraint and delegated more tasks to Henry and Rob.

Almost nobody noticed the shorter hours the Kon Tikki kept that afternoon.

The Porters were back, and Stanley did not mind sitting next to their table. Nobody seemed to miss the conspicuous absence of the old Kon-Tiki expedition frame.

39 - NEAT FRACTURE

THE OFFICE of the doctor was hidden in the guise of a perfectly normal-looking cottage, among similar neighbors, but the inside had been modified to hold a reception area and an examination room.

"Hold tight."

Dr. Salim was a small-looking man, compared to Josh, but he had a wiry strength and a powerful grip. He wound a gauze band round and round his patient's non-negligible torso. He had one of those short beards that were neatly defined, advantaging his features.

As the amiable doctor had checked the aching places and pressed distinct, arcane points with the delicacy of a woman, his dark eyes missed nothing of Josh's reactions.

That he had made a hole in his schedule was nothing short of miraculous. Rob had pestered him all the previous evening, and finally, he had enrolled Henry to make sure he visited the clinic first thing in the morning. The cook had, uncharacteristically, risen early to offer a lift to get Josh to the clinic.

The doctor had concluded that one rib was broken, a neat fracture.

"How come a break can be clean?" Josh asked, annoyed.

His fingers pressed on his bandaged torso, and he was relieved to feel the dull ache that had replaced he fiery pain.

"Because it's a single crack. Your rib will mend by itself."

"Soo, I just have to wait?"

The doctor fixed his last knot, tightening the binding.

"Yes and come see me in two days to change this bind. And no heavy lifting or work."

Josh was stunned. His parents needed him.

"But, I…"

The shorter doctor pointed an index on his sternum, a tap that he felt throughout. His dark eyes pinned Josh like a butterfly.

"Until your bone is mended, any foolish exertion can break it again, and the splinters would puncture your organs. You wouldn't want to die from internal bleed, do you?"

"So?" Rob asked a few minutes later, when he emerged from the freshly painted white-boarded house. Rob, his apartment not too far from the plush neighborhood, had walked there. "Was it a rib? What did he say?"

Josh gloomed.

"No shenanigans for a few days," he said, looking at his running shoes.

Rob's manga-blue eyes searched his face.

"This calls for a change of plans, big boy," he said.

Josh was still reeling from his forced inaction, but before he could respond, a raspy voice a voice called from the street.

"Hey, boss, you coming?"

Henry's battered VW was waiting at the curb.

Rob sauntered down the path leading to the sidewalk. Josh picked his steps cautiously down the clinic's front stairs, feeling like a frail grandfather.

40 - ERRANDS

When Rob descended from the train at NY North station on a Monday morning, he felt as if the last years had melted, and he was again this lost boy in quest for free booze and food.

The smells, of leather, rusted metal, moist floors, hot sandwiches, mixed with the perfumes, colognes added by humans to mask the pollution.

Stopping under the main arch of the grand, old building, he let the noise of the big city wash over him, so alien after months lived in quiet, quaint Safe Harbor. Cars engine groaning, klaxon blaring, boombox rock songs vibrating from low-roofed sports cars, calls and greeting of the voyagers, and raspy voices of beggars in ragged clothing asking for a *dime, do you have a dime?*

Over the jumble of sounds, Rob heard the velvety sound of a flight of pigeons, probably chased by a raptor, or by an annoyed human.

There had been a time when Rob relished the stampede, the frantic beat, the hurrying from one place to another, the flirting, the action... Now, he was surprised to discover he didn't need that heady concoction anymore.

He sensed a gaze on him, from the columns. He looked sideways, in time to catch an anonymous, hooded head, shadowed face, receding.

Of course, by pausing too long at the station's front steps, Rob had signaled to every pickpocket in the area that he was a wide-eyed tourist. He climbed down the stone stairs. He had enough money in his hidden belt for a cab fare, but he wanted to save as much as he could of his and Mel's pooled money.

He had had rejected Josh's offer of paying to get Rob to his folks in Smithtown. It was not the only thing he had refused. Josh had offered to get him a handgun, but Rob's knowledge of the law and his usual caution won over fear. He couldn't see himself pointing the canon at anyone, not even that stupid lovesick mobster.

There have been a heated discussion about what to do. Even without the rib fracture, Josh would be too conspicuous to make the inquiries about the elusive money. So his big warrior settled for doing what he did best, manage the Kon Tikki for a few days, with the special help of Mel who had taken a few days off her other place.

After checking that his Red Sock cap stayed firmly in place, hiding his red hair, Rob checked the bus map, and took the line for Queens. Then, as the bus passed the restaurant area, he stepped down.

He had wanted to see the place where his love had worked. No kidding, he was in a posh district. Policemen would have stopped him then and there if he had a darker skin. As for now, he took advantage of his reedy frame and youthful appearance to cast glances about.

The district had not changed much since last time. He

found out the address. But no smoking ruins. Instead, two marble columns and a pearl-red brick block rose from a bed of upturned earth and napping bulldozers. The first story was the typical commercial space, with large windows looking off the street. The upper stories had smaller, more function that aesthetic, windows with grey boxes of conditioning units. Office space, probably.

Peering inside, Rob saw that the interior had been remade anew, from who knew what money source.

Boards of renovation permission, and city permits covered one window, from the inside. All were of the right date. Josh had told Rob he sold the lot to the first newcomer. Well, that newcomer certainly knew a lot about the restoration business.

The walls had been painted a cheerful reddish rose, a color that complemented nicely the gold and bronze of the lamps and the wood of the chamfrain panels. Tables were pushed on a side, but they would be more than adequate to the task. High-back chairs were piled on the side. From a door in the back, he could guess the silver and copper metal of the kitchen implements.

The building up was completed, and a bord stamped in the ground promised a new dining experience under a new administration.

He did not want to linger in this place. Some of the thugs might be haunting the premises, hoping that someone,—the true murderer?—betrayed himself or herself by trying to get inside.

Rob had another errands to care, an errand that called for his rusty knowledge. As Josh ignored the business structure, he would have to consult the incorporation archives for the five previous years. If the restaurant had been made into a corporation by Rafe, and somehow the bastard had filled papers for the necessary annual meetings without even telling Josh, there would be a trace in public records. If it was a limited partnership, with one partners at the risk of losing his shirt for the other's debts (a concept that Josh grasped), he would also be able to access the records, the same with a LLC, where every partner was protected in a shit-hitting-the-fan case.

The name lists could be accessed from any government website, something Rob could have done from his sister's home computer. However, the recent experience to the tender mercies of the mob had made him wary at exposing his modest self.

So Rob chose an Internet café, entered with his cap on, paid his due, and sat at the rear, between two very entranced *Warcraft* players in real-time strategy game. He spent exactly two seconds regretting his own playing sessions as a student, then, he set to work on the keyboard.

In five minutes, he found his answer. He sat back, stunned. He had expected : the LLP, the LP, bad news, or finding nothing, which meant the business was a gentlemen's agreement. He had not expected the confirmation that *The Lucky Traveler Fine Restaurant* had been incorporated with only Raphael Giordano as CEO, Josh's name only appearing in the list of the CA, as some employees. When he discussed the restaurant, Josh had said he had been happy to sign any paper Rafe had presented him. Minutes of CA meetings that poor, overworked Josh never attended.

What Josh didn't understand was that the corporation was its own separate entity, with its own, distinct flow of money and tax returns. Easy to set up an empty shell company that would funnel the ill-acquired gains. Easy also to wash ill-gained money...

Of course, the family must have been through the company's accounts, make the same reasoning, and found *nada*.

Hence their relentless pursuit of Josh.

Rob read down, finding a date of change of direction. Two months after the fire, the ownership of the company had passed to the Giordano's younger son.

He wanted the signatures on it, because only Josh could, as the last CA member, allow this change. He found a badly printed scan on the screen, with a hazy signature in blue ink, purposely from Josh Tallgate.

And two other signatures, which he surmised were Rafe's younger flames. He explored the news archives to get some hands-on info about the fire.

He carried on more pedestrian errands, food among those, before hopping on the Long Island bus.

Rob curled himself over a lone seat on the upper deck and let the landscape flow by him while the big diesel engine hummed along. The double decker would carry him over the Interstate 495 in direction of Smithtown.

The pervasive scent of nylon and polyamid fabric coating the seats danced around him, along with the nose-tingling recycled air and a heavy perfume worn by a rail-thin blonde. He could smell the alcohol breath from another fellow passenger three rows back.

He rested, making sure no part of his papers or cards was easily reachable. Until he woke up, hundreds of kilo-meters later, rested. He thought about the affair.

Two years was quite a short time to get approval and construct. He supposed the family of the former owner –

Rafe – had shown up and powered up the remaining CA to sign off the ownership.

He wondered if Rafe had made a will. If the older man had hidden his liaison with Josh from his family, he may have bequeathed his other possessions to someone else. Who was getting the big house, for instance?

But then, the murder brought in perspective the danger. He would do Josh's errand, and then a few snooping of his own.

The resolve felt so good he slept all the way to the Smithville stop.

THE PEOPLE VISITING the big Apple had no idea that so much of the countryside was made of a string of villages whose stories where intimately linked with the big history.

Smithville, according to the legend, had been founded by a John Smith whose main claim to fame was to have saved a chief's daughter's life. In exchange, the father would give the new arrivals as much land as he could circle with an ox, in a single day. The guy would snatch a pretty strip of land, considering he chose the summer solstice day.

As Rob stood next to the statue of the bull in question, surrounded by grass and flowers, he thought about savvy guys and gals. He would have to be more than savvy to get Josh off his predicament, even if, for now, he hadn't have a clue.

41 - THE FOLKS

THE ADDRESS JOSH had given him was of a smallish one-story wooden bungalow that looked like a postcard, surrounded by a profusion of flowering bushes that helped forget the smallness of the lot. Similar smallish pastel-colored houses lined the street, remote enough from the downtown area to be almost quiet.

A lively band of sparrows disputed the bread crumbs falling from his sandwich, the birds petulant, tweeting arrogantly, while some mourning doves were perched on the electric lines, cooing down their beak from their moral high point.

He made his way to the front porch, surveying the calm street for suspicious cars. He found none. He checked the corner, the sidewalks, without finding any threat more serious than a boy running after his (unleashed) golden retriever.

The house was protected by a yellow and red sticker from some three-letters alarm company, promising a prompt response should anyone enter the premises. Rob suspected the whole protection was the sticker itself. A metal screen door was closed over a white entrance door. He tested the screen door handle: the unsafe lock was in place.

He took a steadying breath, and, after another look at the neighborhood, pushed the pearly button.

A ten-note carillon sounded inside the house. Then, lively steps came to the door. Lock unlatching.

Hinges groaned as the door was pulled a crack, just enough for a pair of dark eyes to peer at the visitor, using the sliding lock to prevent a force entrance.

"We're not interested!" a woman's voice said.

Rob had not announced himself, sharing Josh's fear of listening devices.

"I'm not a salesman," he said, sliding his fingers in the opening before the woman pushed the door close.

"You all say that," she said. "Funny how no one is a vendor anymore. You're all counselors, associates, and what."

She made to push the door back, ending the conversation.

"Get your hand off, mister, or you'll lose those fingers!"

Rob complied, as he found his *Sesame* phrase.

"I'm a friend of Josh," he said as the door slammed shut.

Stupid, he berated himself. Should have stated my business instead of disputing his salesman statute.

He waited, and stepped down, one stair, two stairs. How could he admit to Josh failing this errand? He fingered the thin phone. Using it would put him on the mobster's map.

As he stood there, fidgeting, a gardener came from the side of the house, in knee-length shorts, one trowel in hand. Tight-curled gray hair escaped from a *Bert's Garage* orange hat. The man was of medium height, and wiry, but the sharp planes of his face, even burdened by the years, carried a striking resemblance to his son. *He must have been quite a knocker in his youth*, Rob thought.

The gardener squinted under his cap, surveying Rob.

"You know Josh?" he asked.

The man pulled his hand and took him to the back-yard. The backyard was on the small side, but two fruit trees, a row of tomatoes and beds of peonies lend beauty and color to the limited space.

"He's no salesman, Ruthie," he called through the screen door.

A woman came out of the spring door, draped in a light, flowery dress, her thick mane of hair pulled back in a loose bun. Rob could appreciate her chocolate eyes, and the arched eyebrows she had bequeathed her hunky son.

ONCE HIS IDENTITY as a genuine friend of Josh was established, the Tallgates opened their door and their heart to this unknown young man.

Rob secretly suspected that the Fixer guy might have used this same ruse (*"Hey, I'm a friend of Rafe"*) to check on them, but the joy in the couple's faces told him how starved they were for news of their sons' whereabouts.

"Let me take your things," Ruth said as she ushered him by the spring door.

He stepped on a tiled floor, and a smell of roasting chicken floated along with herbs. He could see herbs pots lined against the window, and more pots and pans hanging from a rack over the bright yellow wall.

He dropped his rucksack on the floor and lifted off the cap, letting his damp red curls dangle.

"You must be thirsty, will all this heat!"

In a moment, Rob was seated at a pine table shone, the effect of layers of varnish, setting off the red woven table mats, and the blue, blue ceramic plates on it. A tall glass of lemonade landed on a coaster made from the same women fabric. Josh's dad was not worried about his threat level, because he had gone back to his gardening outside.

He took a sip. The lemon and sugar tasted brought him back to his mother's house, as a child. With real, house-made lemonade, with a touch of mint leaves swimming in the pitcher. She had served a similar portion to her husband, then endeavored to make room for a third plate and mat.

"You came just at the right time for dinner," she said.

Rob felt himself blushing. He regretted the cloak-and-dagger way to approach Josh's folks.

"I'm sorry," he said. "I should have called, but…"

Ruthie waved away his concerns.

"Nonsense," she said. "We don't get a lot of visits since… well, since Josh left."

Her voice had caught after the since. Then she covered it by bustling around, breaking eggs, adding milk, flour, beating the mix into a syrupy batter.

He breathed in the cooking chicken, and the garden's green, clean smell coming by the back window.

"So, she asked, how is he?"

He's well, he has opened a restaurant in my town, and the mobsters are after him because his boyfriend stole money from them. Of course, Rob couldn't say that.

"He's OK, but he misses his friend, Rafe," he said.

She paused, pouring the batter into a mold.

"We miss him, too. Such a generous man!" she said.

Josh's dad came back, with a small basket of fresh-picked tomatoes, smelling ripe. As Rob stood to leave them some space, his gaze fell over a framed photography, on the wall facing the window. The yellows had faded with the sun exposure, but enough reds, greens and blues had stayed.

On it, Josh's parents in Sunday clothes, seated at a dining table with a forest of crystal glasses, water and wine pitchers, silver cutlery winking. Between them, a striking silver-haired man, one hand resting lightly over each parent's shoulder. The man was wearing a adjusted suit, with a glossy silken tie, dark red.

His wide smile seemed to lit up the room, as his pale gaze was directed toward the photographer. Ms. Tallgate's motherly face was beaming.

"Rafe?" he asked.

The mother turned, batter bowl in the crook of her arm. Her dark eyes fogged behind her glasses.

"Yes," she said. "He was good to our son. Such a horrible tragedy!"

Rob did not share the doting mother's concern, but something in the gentleman's features felt odd. He had seen this face before.

Yes, on a magazine, at his sister's flat. The unresolved case, baffling the police. *The murder still unsolved*. Rob looked closer, because there was something in this man's carefree attitude that felt familiar.

"Do you have another picture of him?" he asked.

Her eyes went moist.

"Oh, we gave much of those to that nice mister Fix, for Rafe's dad."

Rob's shoulders deflated.

"But wait, she said. The was that magazine, the other day… Go in the salon *(she waved the wooden spoon in the passage)* it should be on the rack."

THE SALON WAS a prim and docile room decked in all shades of blue and white: pale drapes to the front window, blue sofa and chairs, with violet cushions, cream-colored long-haired carpet where any leftover crumbs would stand out like a pimple on a teen's face. The room was a reception area, two side tables and a low coffee table, but it was clear to him that the kitchen was the real meeting place for the Tallgates.

He localized a wicker basket offering a pile of magazines.

The upper most was the same issue of the McCleans he had seen at Mel's flat. The Godfather-style guy with sunglasses. This time he read the names. This time, he sat down and flipped through the glossy pages.

There was a full feature article inside, with more glossy pictures of the deceased. He latched onto a picture of Rafe standing next to a footballer-size hunk with a dark mane of hair, at he restaurant opening. Josh with hair, a young chef proving his mettle in the New-York high dining scene.

By Jove, but his big warrior had looked regal, with this dark mane escaping the white chef bonnet!

And so happy, next to the man he loved… Maybe still loved, in a rueful, guilty way. A tiny, uninvited jealousy peeked in him. He peered closer to the picture.

Rafe's wavy, silver hair ignited something in Rob.

He peered at the other pics. One had the tall

gentleman leaning against a concrete pillar, with a background of many bodies engaged in dancing in a wide loft. The costume he was wearing was a cross breasted jacket with David Bowie-style lapels over a white shirt. The tie was one of those thin violet striped things.

Recognition dawned. The wide lapels jacket had bee ripped in the brawl, and blood spotted his pristine shirt under the loosened tie.

That cool silver fox type who had defended Rob and got clobbered, who had helped him up, his white shirt tainted with red blotches from his bleeding nose, who had pressed a hundred bill in his hand, before turning back to the hunk...

This is a cosmic joke, he thought.

He *had* met Josh's love. And maybe, that big hairy hunk had been Josh.

"Dinner's ready," a light voice called out.

He let the magazine drop and stood. As he walked the length of the yellow-walled passage toward the warm smell of spices and chicken, he smiled inwardly.

Well, that proves that Josh and I share the same good tastes.

42 - MINDING THE BUSINESS

JOSH PLACED the print black and white copy showing the original Kon-Tiki crew on its crochet.

"You sure that name's not brand-protected?" Melody asked. "You know, like those Disney cartoon characters?"

The young woman had readily accepted filling in the position for a short time. It hadn't taken long to guess that she was as business-savvy as her brother.

"Nope," he said. "Thor Heyerdahl never took out a trademark for 'Kon-Tiki'. But many others did."

"Well," Mel said, "I guess it was for the best. 'Cause a copyright infringement suit can be expensive."

Josh nodded. There were tons of 'Kon-Tiki' bars and restaurants around the world, trademarked or not. This kind of easy-going place was as remote from the high-brow *Lucky Traveler* as could be. He had counted on Rafe's family concentrating its searches on the more uppity establishments who would readily hire a talented chef. It would have worked, except for the curse of social medias. He couldn't simply *stop* being a good chef.

"Hello! How are you?"

Mel was greeting a young woman in pink walking on the promenade, a baby carrier slung to her back. Among the throngs of tourists, Josh recognized her because of the pink dress. The young mother looked like a faded postcard form the fifties, except for the modern baby carrier. She had no make up, neither lipstick on her. As she paused near the bamboo posts of the terrace, Mel engaged the conversation about raising a child.

Like her brother, she was easygoing and engaging. For the last two days of replacing her brother, Melody Sundance had shown initiative and spunk. Josh suspected his restaurant's earnings would be higher, but he was too anxious about Rob's errand to give her all his attention.

He stepped inside the kitchen to get the evening meal ready. Not Henry's colored cursing at the indifferent Thermidor could lift his load of worries.

43 - HALF OF THE ANSWER

THE MEAL, and the company, proved excellent. The hanging herbs and the garden's air felt a total change from Safe Harbor's seashore smells.

The parent's wary attitude at the stranger had melted, but Rob refrained from mentioning his own feelings towards their son, not wanting to muddle the water of this simple, friendly relationship. He missed his own parents, and the easy atmosphere that had reigned when he had been very small. There might have been a similar carefree atmosphere, he thought.

The dinner conversation flowed naturally, from the food, from the weather. Rob gently prodded them about their immigration in the US, and their relatives still in New-Zealand.

In return, they grilled him about Josh's whereabouts. After the fire, they saw their son once, and afterwards, only got postcards, from various places in the world. *Don't tell them yet*, had been Josh's instruction. The vandalism and threats had racked up Josh's protectiveness toward his parents.

"He will tell you himself, soon," Rob promised, between two mouthfuls of chicken.

The parent's anxious faces tugged at him. The meal congealed in his stomach. He promised himself to make sure they would get to see their boy.

They also wanted to know was their son happy? Did he work at a restaurant at his new place?

Rob gave them a double yes, erring on the cautious side of truth. As Ruth filled the porcelain sink, he rose and naturally pulled a side drawer, taking a dry clothe. Ruth looked at him with awe.

"All kitchens are similar," Rob said.

Josh's mother gratefully accepted his help for cleaning the dishes.

He went on the scenario Josh had proposed, of telling about an old bank account he might have forgotten at their place. Could he see Josh's old room?

By then, Ruthie, mellowed by the way he cleaned the dishes, and stacked them up, would have given him the moon.

In the bungalow, the second room had been Josh.

"He lived here before he went to the Culinary Institute," his dad said.

"But he visited in the weekends and we left that room untouched."

Seeing the room did not provoke any particular emotion in Rob. He liked, no, *loved* Josh, but the teenage boy things, posters, sports memorabilia, triangular fanons, left him cold. Rob found, however, a collection of old paper *Shonen Jump* before they went electronic only, and other, smallish manga books stacked on a shelf. He flipped through some collections, surprised to find a giant-sword-wielding, redhaired boy on a cover.

"Did Rafe visited here?" he asked, pulling drawers.

"No, Josh never brought him here," Ruthie said.

The dresser was empty of clothes, probably donated. Rob had hoped to find some scrap of paper, some note Josh would have made and quickly forgotten, him not being the bean counter type.

"You're not the first going through his things," the father said.

He guessed as much, and that the parents might have tidied the place after the family men went through Josh's things. He wasn't sure if he could find more, but he took the time to flipped the pages of all the manga books.

It's incredible how many improvised page markers could be found into books. He got some tickets to the Mets, to Broadway and some other pricey entertainment venues. After more fruitless research, Rob went back to the kitchen. Again, he passed the framed photograph.

He sat on the back porch, enjoying the cool summer evening. He would have to make his way back, find an hostel, but for now, he needed to stay put, look at the sky slowly turning a rosy skin tone marked by passing plane contrails, and think.

Josh had pondered what Rob should say to his parents.

But the idea of shuffling off this nice couple away from their garden, and condemn them to a life of hiding like a witness protection program but minus the protection, grated at his conscience.

He would find a way.

"Mister Sundance?"

Rob turned, to find the old proud Maori face looking at him from the garden. The senior Tallgate held a shovel full of granulated compost, the bits of banana peel distinct, and let it fall in a dark rain over the row of vegetables.

"Yeah?"

"Is our boy in trouble?"

Rob started. How could Tallgate have known?

But then, some parents had a sixth sense to smell when something was amiss. So, more tea was involved in the cheery kitchen as he told them about the new restaurant in Safe Harbor.

Now that the mobsters knew where to find Josh, better his folks knowing, too. Rob gave them a toned down account of the vandalism act, and the threats against him, without getting into any details, except that it had a relation with Rafe's death. He didn't mention the missing money.

As he spoke, he saw how the husband's hands crept to his wife's, while his hooded eyes kept riveted to the guest.

"We... gathered as much when Rafe was killed and Josh disappeared," he said. "Mister Fix came to pay us a visit."

"Bringing those horrid white flowers," Ruthie added, frowning. "I could see something was off. He was looking for something. Like drugs, or I don't know."

"It wasn't drugs," Rob said. "Josh's clean as a fresh washed shirt."

Rob had the pleasure of seeing the reassurance in her eyes. How they had worried in those years!

He yawned, the measure of the day on him.

"Got to go," he said rising.

Ruthie protested.

"There's no bus leaving this late in the weekday. You can sleep here and get the bus tomorrow," she said.

"I, I don't want to intrude," Rob said, dismayed.

But Josh's mom was already opening a wardrobe and pulling out folded bedsheets. Feeling tired to the bones, Rob gratefully took up the offer.

Soon, he had showered and was lying in Josh's bed.

A NATURAL NEED prodded Rob to the bathroom. As he came back, he couldn't refrain from examining the picture in the kitchen.

It was two in the morning, a small lamp was giving off a faint light. He took down the frame, and brought it in the room, closing the door, turning up the light.

He turned the framed picture of the parents with Rafe. It was your everyday print with a black cardboard back, thick, a dark wood frame, a spacing frame and a glass protection.

He removed the print. Under it, he found a strip of yellowed Chinese biscuit paper. Over the ill-printed savvy saying of *the half of my love keeps you warm,* the paper bore four digits and three letters. Many Chinese cookie slips suggested lucky lotto numbers. However, those letters and numbers were not lottery numbers.

The letters were the transit code for a Geneva bank, well-known for trading in all kinds of secret accounts. The numbers identified the account. However, it was incomplete: only one half of the numbered account.

Where was the other half?

On the bright side, he had gotten an answer. The hidden account existed. In there, would be the laundered money, stashed away by Rafe. Maybe that crafty gentleman had had in mind to give a hint to Josh at a later point, but he got killed before he could.

∾

ROB TOOK his leave in the morning, not without receiving *mucho* kisses from Josh's mother, to transmit to his friend. During the time he spent there, both parents had seen through his "concerned friend" charade, and Rob's expression had let them guess the extent of his feelings for their son.

Her parting words had strengthened the resolve to see this sordid enigma to its end.

"We miss our Joshua so much, it burns me."

He made sure no lipstick remained on his cheek before leaving.

In the metrobus, Rob fingered the slip of paper.

He had maintained radio silence, but in his shoulder bag was one long letter form his mother's hand, probably written during the night while Rob was dismounting (and re-mounting) their framed picture.

44 - FINAL ACCOUNT

THE KON TIKKI kitchen was cooling off after another hectic day. The hum of the metal gray freezer and the refrigerator had rose to prominence as the other shops closed and the excited conversations dwindled down. The ambient air, too, had cooled. Josh sat on a folding chair, his back to the treacherous Thermidor oven, his large shoulders wrapped in his hoodie.

Rob had explained his discovery again, to Josh.

"So, the good news is, there was a secret stash," he said.

Henry had left, but Melody had insisted to stay, pretexting to drive Rob home after.

Melody was hugging her brown cashmere pull around her, the dark color setting off her flaming hair.

"If I understand what my bro told you, boss," she said, "we have two days to find the rest of this account number."

Josh raised his arms, palms up. He seemed annoyed that she had been let in the loop, but Rob knew he could not prolong the charade indefinitely to his small sister. Not if those mobsters could off him any time. He had opened like a book and told her everything, after her battered Volvo had put-putted to get him at the Fallsworth terminal.

Josh shifted, feeling the bandage around his ribs.

"I told you," he said, his voice heavy with weariness. "I left everything in my parents' home. Most of what I have in my flat here has been bought a few months ago, when I came here to rent the space at the pier."

Rob looked around.

"Nothing in this kitchen, then, that Rafe would have given you? No special gift?"

Josh shrugged, pulling his cotton hoodie closer to him.

"Not even a spoon," he said, glum. "There's nothing coming from my friend here. No papers, no…"

He stopped, his dark eyes unfocused, fingers clutching at the fabric.

"There's just this pullover," he said. "He gave it to me before I left for the business trip. So I would think of him each time I wore it."

Josh pulled out the hoodie, with slow moves to avoid hurting his ribs.

Rob fingered it. The thick cotton pull had came from a fancy Gap store, according to the label. The price tag had been ripped, of course, but Rob guessed it must have been name-expensive.

He stretched the pull on the work table.

Rob and Melody each passed their hands on the cloth, feeling on each long sleeve, checking the double lining of the hood. Melody held the pull in front of the kitchen light fixture, and the pull fibers appeared like like an X-Ray. No creases of Chinese cookie paper inserted there.

At last, Rob had to admit no slip of paper had been

sewn in the hood, no secret pocket resided there. He handed the gray sweater to his boss.

"I am sorry, Josh," he said. "I'm so sorry."

"Well," Melody said. "At least you have a part of it."

Rob shook his head.

"Mel, I'm not sure those men will accept less than the full account. Plus, there's no guarantee the money's still there."

She crossed her arms.

"Then, where are they supposed to meet you?"

45 - THE DON

THE INSIDE of the limousine felt like a living room to Josh, with the leg room, the cow leather cushioning, the minibar. The car itself was humming softly, if not for the radio playing on the car's speakers. The audio quality was top-notch, but the insipid pop songs did not deserve such quality. The ventilator spewed a cold breath of conditioned air on his neck that barely atoned for the torrid Cologne worn by the Fixer.

He huddled more into his gray sweater. He had parted with his best penguin suits years ago, and had decided to go with his customary black jeans and black Tee. If he was to die tonight, at least he would do so in comfortable clothes.

The Fixer was sitting on the opposite bench, apparently entranced by the *Jack Reacher* paperback he was reading. Josh had considered overpowering the thin man who was reading his novel as if he was in a barber shop, waiting for his turn. But this would not help.

There was no conversation, since Josh had refused the offer of drinks. It was too stymied by the "last drink of the condemned" joke that one of the Fixer's men had spouted as they went in. The two thugs that had beaten him were in the car, too. One driving, with the sappy love tunes, the other in the passenger seat.

They had less than five hours of road to contemplate the end.

He tried to look outside the tainted windows, but the night had stolen the landscape they were passing. Only flashes of yellow, orange, red lights of cars passing by with a dampened engine drone, and the occasional blue and red flash of ambulances or police cars, but the limo driver was driving under the speed limit.

He looked down.

Rob's head was a slight weight on his knees, his red mane freshly washed. He passed a cautious hand over the hair, but Rob did not even stir. The young man had leaned against him like an overburdened tree, and soon had passed out in exhaustion.

No wonder, Josh thought.

The last thirty-six hours had been filled with serving clients and frantic search in his flat, and calls to his parents (there was no point in hiding). Rob had spent long hours over his sister's screen, poring over banking websites and police websites. Mel's computer hadn't turned up new evidence, except for the Geneva-based bank. The papers were full of speculations about the celebrities using this institution, but no solid clue. Asking nicely about a client's number was out of the question. Josh had no way to even know under what name the account had been set up.

They hadn't gone to the police, fearing the mobster's retribution on Josh's parents. He dropped his gaze to encompass his dear elf's face, his parted lips so much like the first time Josh had seen him. He should have taken his insulin before getting in the car, but he had decided against it, stating he would need his full head later.

Rob had insisted to come with him, even if the mobsters had not asked for him. Josh was angry at first, because the younger man was putting his life in danger, for what amounted to a mad gamble. But a part of him --that he tried his best not acknowledging-- was secretly pleased that Rob had not abandoned him.

As they rolled closer to their destination, the series of turns and stops navigating the streets woke up Josh's companion, who was rubbing his eyes.

"Are we there, yet?" Rob asked, with the childish tone that drew a reluctant smile from Josh.

The younger man yawned and stretched out like a lazy cat, his feet touching the fixer's pants, which caused the mobster to shy back with a snarl.

"Stand back, you dolt!" he said. "The Don doesn't care much for your kind!"

"As you would know," Josh said.

The snarky response made him feel better. After all, what difference did it make, if he was fated to die this night?

THE LIMOUSINE SPIT them off the curb in a swanky, well-lit district. Looking around, Josh recognized the neighborhood of his former restaurant, except that a new glass-paned monster rose from the ashes of the Lucky Traveler.

Rob had spilled out his opinion about the celerity of the reconstruction. He had no doubt that major threads had been pulled.

The restaurant of the first floor was now open, the tall

windows showing white-clad servers doing the rounds. However, all the tables were empty.

THE DON's table had been set a in room looking over the Hudson river. With a mild shock, Josh noticed how the disposition of the space was close to the VIP room of the *Lucky Traveler*. A wave of nostalgia hit him, as he recalled his mom and dad, with Rafe's hands resting on their shoulders, the silver fox looking inordinately pleased with himself.

Josh's gaze roamed over the silver cutlery, the linen napkins, the tubular glasses, crystal no doubt. This could be their last meal. As a chef, he saw everything could be made into a weapon, except the rounded butter knifes. He stomach groaned as he couldn't help identifying the dried tomatoes and spices of the *Minestrone* prepared in the kitchen, and the enticing garlic bread heating in the oven. A tinkling of cooking pots, the softer thuds of wood ladles, the hiss of boiling water, all linked by curd orders given in *sotto voce*, hinted at a frantic activity.

He hoped the new restaurant's chef would prove be equal to the challenge.

A not-too-gentle push between his shoulder blades prodded him forward. The blond goon pulled a chair, one place remote from the head of the table. Where the Don would sit, a fine set of cutlery was spread, with a ice bucket holding a bottle of (my god, was it possible?) Moet&Chambon, the year not visible from his position.

Champagne to celebrate.

Rob's opinion had prevailed over Josh, in that they would say they had something. It was a gamble. He could feel with his fingers the slip of Chinese cookie paper crumpled in the kangaroo pocket of his hoodie. The men had searched them before ushering them in the limo that appeared by magic at the meeting point, near the old fish plant.

Rob was placed opposite to him, also one empty chair remote from the table's end. The higher end, from the Middle Age kings' tables. With his orange Tee-Shirt sporting a manga-looking striped gray cat, his elf looked out of place at this white-clothed table.

The Fixer took the empty chair between Rob and the table's head. For now, they were only three at the table, but four well-dressed men were stationed like black and white statues at the door they had passed, and at another door, that had not been in the original design. His sight aligned on the jackets, searching for the tell-tale bulge of firearms. He skin of his arms pricked at the images rising in his head, and instead, he concentrated on the portion of the Hudson that he could see from his place, between Rob and the Fixer.

A white-clad attendant came in and distributed menus tall, leather bound menus. Rob propped the menu open in front of him, so his face was hidden, except for the top curls of his red hair showing. Josh went rapidly over the two panels. If this was their last meal, as well choose the best.

He was so focused on the offerings, that he did not heed the other door opening, the reverent whispers, the low-toned drone of an electric engine, until the wheelchair bearing Don Giordano was halfway to the chair-less head of the table.

The Fixer had jumped to his feet.

"Rise," he said.

Josh obeyed, dazed. Rafe had brought the Don only once at his restaurant, around Christmas; he kept the memory of an older, elegant gentleman with a soft voice, moving with elaborate caution, barely leaning his weight on his dark cane.

At fist, Josh barely recognized the thin husk propped up against the cushions of the wide dossier, lost in a mid-gray suit the wide lapels. The Don had aged in two years, and only his wavy silver hair were styled. His gaunt face was a blur of vertical and diagonal lines, his neck hung in cords under the perfect knot of the tie. He smelled of Cologne, maybe to hide more failing bodily functions.

But his voice had kept the iron will of his leadership under the velvety-soft glove.

"Lets it, first, my children," he said, his pale gray eyes surveying the table from their recessed cavern.

The Don's pale gray eyes were so much like his nephew's that Josh had an awkward impression of a very old Rafe. His breath caught. Of course, now he would never know how growing old together would be.

46 - FAMILY DINNER

Rob checked his tee shirt as the elegant head of the Giordano family entered.

Talk about under-dressing, he thought.

But he had insisted to accompany Josh. And he felt best in his good old U orange tee shirt, dating from a more innocent time, when he thought his avenues open. The heat had been ratcheted up, in regard for the old man sitting at the table.

Now he looked as maybe twenty attendants danced around the old Don, bringing this and that, and he felt as a extra in a mafia movie.

An extra that could be dispatched in the next scene. Well, he *had* insisted to come, didn't he?

While they were choosing their meals, new members of the family had taken place, silent as black suited phantoms.

Two men in their forties bearing a family resemblance with the Don and Rafe sat at the other end of the table, their fingers clinking with rings. They might have been regulars at the Traveler: a flash of recognition passed in their brown eyes as they saw Josh's massive figure a the table.

And there were two other men, young and white and impeccably dressed. Their eyes kept darting about, as if they were in a fairy-tale ballroom. Impressed to be honored guests at the Don's family table.

Those Cinderellas looked like what the police documents called "hopefuls".

They would be the ones ending up killing them, not the Fixer's goons. New hard menus flopped around.

Then they ordered, Rob choosing a *médaillon de veau* with red wine sauce and peas. Josh went for a red West Coast salmon slices in white cheese and pesto sauce, with sticky rice.

The Don did not need to make his wishes known.

A waiter brought a steaming plate of soup smelling of ripe tomatoes and tarragon. He lowered the soup on the white cloth with the caution of a lunar landing. A tiny nod of the silver head acknowledged his satisfaction.

During the course of the meal, Rob noticed how his big warrior cast side glances at the Don. *Like a sheep hoping to gain the wolf's confidence*, he thought.

No, that was not it. His Josh was seeing something fascinating in the old man who would kill them.

Then, the pics he had pored over on the Internet came back to his mind. The old Don looked like an older, craftier Rafe. He should have seen it earlier, but he had his eyes on the Fixer. Josh had been right, the man was hiding a secret.

Then, as he couldn't do else, Rob focused on the tasty meat.

∾

THE MEAL WAS OVER TOO FAST for Josh, who stared at the home-made gelato, rising like a pale tortuous ghost from the crystal bowl. He took a cautious spoonful, expecting to hate it, but his taste buds betrayed him, crying out in delight.

He had to admit the new chef was good.

Maybe fear had prevented him to focus on the small talk between the Don and his sons. Both were married, both with a brood of children who would someday partake in the family business.

Suddenly Josh felt a fleeting compassion for the well-prepped sons. They were not that much older than Josh himself, but the price they paid to walk in their father's bloody footsteps showed: one son's hairline was receding, and the other had turned prematurely gray. Tension lines etched their otherwise generous lips.

There's something to be said for leading an honest life, Josh thought.

Then, the empty desert plates were whisked off by the ghost-silent waiters. Only men, Josh noticed.

He felt the burning gaze of the Don on him. The old man daubed his lips, then cleared his throat.

"I believe, Mister Joshua Tallgate, that you have something to tell me."

Rafe had prompted Josh on the etiquette. He pushed his chair and rose, keeping his hands on the white fabric of the tablecloth.

"I do," he said. "Don Giordano, Most honored Sons Luigi and Pietro Giordano, and lieutenant Johannes Fixi, enforcers Jim and…"

He etched a small head bow at each name, none of which he had cared to remember at the restaurant. But his elf had drilled in his head the family's names, from the news and police records.

He even named Carlio and Gepetto, the new comers, from the pics he had made himself study. *The more you show how respectful you are, the more you can get from them*, Rafe had said.

And it worked, as short gasps echoed around the table. A smile even crept on the old Don's face as Josh finished.

"I can see that that scoundrel has taught you well," he said.

Josh nodded.

"First," he said, "I would like to extend my compliments to your new chef. I was dubious at first, but it seems you have found a worthy replacement," he said.

False modesty did not sit well with the Don, another tidbit harvested from his pillow talks.

"However," he added on a lighter tone, "I did not have the pleasure of meeting him."

He topped this sweet declaration with a generous smile. He caught a surprised expression from Rob, who seemed to wonder *speaking about food, now*?

But it had proved a wise choice, because the older, grayer son suddenly beamed like a lighthouse. He half-rose, looked at the Don, who nodded assent, and called.

"Come, Carlotta!"

Josh turned, to see the tall and trim silhouette under the high bonnet.

"Carlotta had graduated from the Culinary Institute," the father said, proud.

Hoping his ribs would not protest, Josh bent lower.

"Miss Giordano, it is a pleasure to meet you," he said. "I had the best meal in years, and this place will be well-served by your talent."

The lady in question blushed. She looked in her high twenties, but had no ring on her finger. Maybe the Don kept her for a special alliance.

"T-Thank you, mister. My father thought highly of you," she added.

The Don's raspy voice interrupted the exchange.

"You can get take the nigh off, Carlotta. And your gelato was a wonder."

As the young woman steps receded, one of the men shut the door behind her leaned against the panel. The soft slam in his back sent a shiver down Josh's spine. Now things would proceed fast.

"So," the Don said, a question and order in one single syllable.

Josh noticed the table had been cleared while he was chatting with the young chef.

"Esteemed Don Giordano, we found out evidence that offshore account Raphael had created exist. It is located in a branch of the Geneva International Transit Bank…

A sucked in breath, from the Fixer. The Don smiled, showing his perfect dentures.

"And the number?" he asked.

Josh took a breath. Rob's hands were interlaced on the white cloth, as in a prayer.

"The account number is 1, 97, 20, 4…"

"Not so fast!" one of the sons said, scribbling madly on a napkin.

Josh repeated the sequence of numbers.

The son who had been writing down looked expectantly at him. *Here it comes*, Josh thought.

"The remaining digits are missing from the paper Raphael had left me."

The declaration brough a storm of exclamations, that the Don quelled, with one gnarly hand.

"May I see this paper, please?"

Josh fished in his kangaroo pocket (happy that he had been searched, otherwise the henchmen could imagine a handgun sitting there). He produced the wrinkled, yellowed strip, between his thumb and index. He extended his arm to give it. The Don's man took it, gingerly, and presented his open palm to his boss.

The old man squinted at it.

"That's a Chinese cookie strip," he said. "*The other half of my love keeps you warm,*" he read.

"This is rubbish!" One of the hopefuls, Carlio with the slim moustache, said.

"But the numbers, father!" the son said, holding up a lacquered cellphone. "Those numbers are legit, and they do correspond with Geneva branch. I just checked. Let me see it."

So the paper passed, while Josh racked his brains. Why would Rafe hid an ordinary paper under the print portrait, unless there was a hidden message in it? The younger son had put an jeweller's mini scope on his left eye and was peering at the paper.

Finally, he let the paper down.

"This strip is a false," he said.

"You could have made this up, all of it," the Don right-hand man said.

Josh protested, keeping his voice equal.

"I think Rafe made it," he said.

There was a pause.

A long, ragged breath, full of regret, escaped from the Don's lips. He lifted his hands, palms up, and looked at the slowly melting ice bucket.

"And to say I had this bottle ready for victory," he said.

A long, weary sigh.

"Take them off my sight," he said.

Josh knew the meaning of that phrase. The Don would never soil his mouth with such crude words as *kill them*. They had lost.

47 - HIDDEN GIFT

Rob's heart beat faster. A look at Josh's face had told him what he needed to know. There was maybe one second worth of hesitation after the Don's words.

The men around the table shifted in two dark waves: the sons going to their father, the hopefuls and bodyguards converging towards Josh. Rob felt the Fixer's hand grabbing his arm, right on the boat tattoo, the nails biting in his skin. *That would leave a trace*, he thought, before wrapping his mind around the new problem.

The Fixer's head came close to his own; Rob wondered if he would kiss him like in those movies, but the man's lips parted to let a low *I'm-sorry-boy* out.

Josh extended his long arms sideways, like a crucified pose.

"*WAIT!*" his friend called out. "Before leaving your presence, I have a last gift for you."

Rob didn't like the expression in his warrior's eyes. And why was he pussy-footing around the fact they would be killed? What was he about to do? What kind of gift could he offer, with all the goons ready to throw them in the Hudson, or in a landfill somewhere?

He chased those thoughts to focus on his big warrior. The older son, standing near his father, had turned, intrigued.

"I can't bring Raphael back," Josh said. "But I can tell you the wonderful things that he had taught me. Not about money making, that's not my talent."

A few chuckles from the sons.

"We ain't got all night," one of the hopefuls said, doing his best to hide his mounting excitement.

"No, you haven't," Josh said. "I am aware of the family's ways. So I won't take much of your time."

The big man wrapped his arms against the warm brushed cotton hoodie, the last trace of Rafe in his life. Then he looked at the Don, now framed between his own burly enforcers.

"Don Giordano, Rafe was your favorite nephew. You doted on him; know that it was reciprocal. Never has he, in the years that I have known him, expressed anything but respect and devotion to his uncle."

Some sniggers, quickly suppressed by the Don's hand slapping on the table.

"Go on," he said, his eyes hooded.

"He, he had his flaws," Josh said, "and yes, his gambling among them, his love of taking risks. Yes, he diverted those millions from the family's accounts. But he always told me he wanted only the best for you. `*They will pardon me once they see how well their funds will have fructified.*`

The Fixer's hand had relented his grasp. Rob made himself as small and inconspicuous as he could in this ocean of aggressive testosterone, while his friend spoke.

"Raphael had told me that he had the intention to

make this money fund grow, and to repay the family after. It was sad that someone took upon himself to punish him for the theft."

The Don eyes had been at mid-mast. They flew open.

"I never gave the order," he said. "Did I, Fixi?"

The Fixer shook his dark head.

"I'd have done it, if you'd asked," he said. "I wouldn't have been happy, though, because he was my pal."

Josh cupped his hands.

"I did my best to find where your money went. Since I can't take Rafe's sweater with me where I'm going, I think it would be best if you kept it. Each time I'm wearing it, I think of him. I hope it will give you back the part of him that you loved."

Josh pulled the hoodie over his head, which enlarged his massive frame.

"Nevertheless, I do hope you find who killed him," he said, his voice muffled. "The police had no clue."

He was clumsy, because the bandage around his waist hindered his moves.

"Let me help him," Rob said, keeping his voice low. "Please," he added.

The Fixer nodded. He followed Rob as the young man skirted the table. Standing on his toes, Rob grabbed the fabric at the waist and pulled up, and Josh wriggled out of the cotton sweater.

As Rob was turning the cloth over to reverse it, his eyes fell over the collar. They had returned the thing and gone over the pockets and lining, but never did they take a close look at the label with the logo and washing instructions.

Now that he was looking at the label, he noticed the row of digits under did not correspond to a corporation number. Two dashes separated the letters from the numbers, and the three first letters formed a bank ID.

"THAT'S IT!"

Rob's happy shout had the henchmen jump back, one's hand going over his belt, but the Fixer's stare stopped him.

He extended the collar between his hands to show the white label.

"Here it is, your Honor!" Rob said. "Here is your *whole freaking account number*! The missing figures are : 9968-9-BW "

A wave of excited whisperings mounted in the room.

"What do you mean?" Josh asked, miffed.

"Don't you remember? He said it!"

Rob felt absurdly right.

"*Half of my love will keep you warm.* That's this top, his last gift to you! A well-crafted label, printed with the logo. I guess Rafe was a good forger when he began his, er, career in the family."

The bespectacled son nodded, as he opened a thin silver computer .

"Yes, he was."

Rob presented the sweater to the closer goon, keeping the collar label in view.

"Take care of it, that's ninety mil worth. Show the label to your boss."

But the older son was already punching madly on his flat computer's keyboard.

"Nine, nine, six, eight, nine, B, W…" he said, biting his lower lip.

Then his eyes popped open.

"I'm on a client access page! It worked!"

A nervous silence followed undercut by the soft tapping of keys.

"Yes, father," he said, pushing his spectacles on the bridge of his nose. "This is an account registered to G. Giordano…"

"Oh!" Rob said. "Not Raphael? Who's that G.?"

A low voice rumbled from the head of the table.

"That would be me, young man. G like Giuseppe Giordano."

The older son raised his hand.

"We're not there, yet," he said. "The full admin access can't be without a secret phrase. The number alone can't give you that."

Rob turned to Josh. The Don was fingering the cloth, like a lost treasure, his eyes blurry.

"I believe the honor of typing the secret phrase goes to the account holder," Rob said. "My guess would be that Chinese biscuit sentence."

Don Giordano blinked, his gaze roaming through Rob's small frame.

"You're quite a resourceful lad," he said. "But what's in it for you? Why did you come here to help your friend?"

He's more than my friend, Rob thought.

"Because," he said, weighting his words, "more than five years ago, your nephew saved me from a bunch of rowdies beating me up. Raphael defended me; he picked me up, he got me money for a taxi. I wouldn't have made it out alive, otherwise."

He felt a boulder forming in his throat as he spoke. He paused, a moment that let him hear the surprised gasp coming from Josh.

"I didn't know his name, then, but I had never forgotten this act of generosity for a low-life he didn't know."

He swallowed.

"This is why I came."

The first son was lowering the computer in front of his father.

Don Giordano typed, squinting, asked in a querulous voice that his son hold the strip of paper straight.

48 - RAFE'S MYSTERY

LATER, they were driven back to Safe Harbor, squeezed on the back seat of a much smaller car than the limo.

"That little guy being beaten up, that *was you*!" Josh hissed. "You should have told me!"

"Well, I, I did not pay attention," Rob said.

Then his mischievous smile came back. "And neither did you see me!"

"Oh, I guess I couldn't fully appreciate your cute face under all that blood!" Josh said, before playfully rolling over his elf's slight frame.

"Well, show some respect for your new financial advisor," Rob said, almost out of breath.

Josh heaved himself up. The shoulder bag was almost bursting with small bank notes, a token of the family's appreciation. The Don had offered him to take on the restaurant as chef, but he had refused, saying he would not insult the talented Carlotta. That answer had set Josh firmly in the good graces of the older son.

"Hiring you had been the best decision of my life," Josh said.

Again, those wide eyes looking at him, dancing with mischief.

"You, big hunk, come closer and I'll show you…"

The driver interrupted them.

"Listen mates, I'm totally OK with you getting a free pass from the Don, I really am, but could you please refrain from doing shenanigans in my fricking *car*?"

The Fixer had been less than pleased at being ordered to drive the guests. But even he had almost lost his supper when the older son announced the amount left in the account.

WITH THE PROPER IDENTIFICATION, Giuseppe and his sons had consulted the records, not expecting much left.

Rafe's gambling losses might have made a dent in the original funds, but his aggressive management and the compounded interests had made the investment soar.

His instructions had been maintained after his death. In two years and a half, the account had flourished to a whopping total of 137,45 millions.

The older son gave Josh a grateful nod.

"Not even our regular long-term deposit could have brought such results," he said, cleaning up his lenses.

The famous champagne bottle was finally popped open.

After glasses of bubbly champagne had made the tour (except for the bodyguards), Josh felt more daring.

"So, esteemed Don, are we off the hook?" he had asked.

The Fixer cast a glance to the Don. "You are, provided you keep mum. If you were to ever babble to anyone about this story, I'll throw the two of you in the sea with concrete boots!"

Nobody laughed, which told Josh they were still serious about their business.

Eventually, they were let out, after the first son had pumped Josh's hand with energy. When Rob and him walked out of the elegant house, following a grumbling Fixer, Josh turned to get a last look at Rafe's and his dream.

EVENTUALLY, in the absence of shenanigans, Rob dozed over his shoulder, the curly red hair tickled his arm. Josh would have to get used to his companion's biological clock. Two glasses of sparking had washed fast over his slight frame. Duly warned, Rob had taken his insulin in the washrooms before the meal. But with the highly emotional meeting, the insulin dose had tapered off before midnight.

Josh was exhausted himself, by the tension and the relief. But he couldn't sleep, thanks to his giddiness over one unresolved issue. They still had two or three hours left before getting to Safe Harbor.

So he stuck a conversation with the man who, a few days ago, had tortured him and threatened Rob.

"Do you have any idea about who killed Rafe? I mean, if not for the millions in the account, then where's the motive?"

The Fixer drove, the yellow and blue LED lampposts coming and going. Josh had decided the hitman was in no mood to answer, when he spoke.

"You see, wild boy, the Don was too taken with his favorite nephew to take him off like that. It's as I told you:

Raphael was tasked to launder the monies, but his moves were not scanned with much attention. He was always saying: *don't worry, it'll come back, it'll come back better*. So the Don had confidence in him."

"But someone else didn't trust him."

Another minute of silence. Those silent types got under Josh's skin.

"Yeah, about that. After our, um, discussion the other day, the Don asked me to look into Rafe's death." He sighed. "Again."

"But is was a mob execution, wasn't it?"

The fixer snorted.

"Nope, wild boy. The goon who offed Rafe had missed a few markers."

"One of his, er, other flames, then," Josh said.

He shifted on the bench, so he wouldn't wake Rob.

"Nope."

"Another gang, then."

"That's the first thing the Don and I checked. None of the other families had even heard about a contract on Raphael. So, no."

Josh was at the end of his wits. He scratched his head, feeling the buzz of new hair growing back. He had neglected to shave in the last days.

"Rafe, he was always good with coming up with schemes. Risky gambles. What if he had done something *else*, beside the secret account, to pay back his gamble debts? Something that the family doesn't know about?"

"There's not a lot of things the family doesn't know about," the Fixer said. "After his death, we discovered he had racked up quite a number of losses at the casinos."

Josh's spirits dropped. That's where Rafe business

meetings had taken him. He could picture his silver fox in the glittering place, dashing, impressing the ladies...

"Oh. But he paid those debts back, didn't he? So it wouldn't be…"

A sudden idea struck him. Rafe, so generous with strangers down on their luck.

"What if he was killed at the restaurant by someone who *owed* him a lot of money?"

The Fixer smiled in the mirror reflection.

"You mean, one of those poor-as-hell losers would hitch a ride and get Rafe to agree to meet, and off him?"

There were no other cars on the road. They were approaching the scattered coastal towns. Between hills or constructions, Josh could see the faint glittering of sea waves struck by the moon light.

The glitter sent Josh to the past, as he envisioned the gratin of NY society stopping at the *Lucky Traveler*, all glittering and sparkling. He had met that crowd, listened to their half-sincere compliments. Starlets, actors and actresses, artists, business tycoons, politicians… all had been under the charm of Rafe's silver tongue.

And Rafe would enthrall more glittering guests at casinos…

I will soon reel in one big fish, he had said.

The suspicions bits and pieces congealed in a hard idea. He cautiously lay Rob,s head on his legs and grabbed the front seat head rest.

"But what if it wasn't a "poor-as-hell" man?" Josh said. "Someone rich or powerful enough, who feared Rafe talking about him, or her? A politician, maybe, caring for his or her reputation?"

This time, the silence stretched longer. The Fixer was

mulling over the possibility. He would have to comb the casinos Rafe had frequented.

"This could take lots of my time," he said. "And cost a bundle."

Josh thought about the pocket money the mobsters had given him. More than enough to repair the damage done to his restaurant. He wasn't ready to part with it yet.

"Yeah, it might be costly," he said. "And, if the culprit could have paid a killer to get Rafe, too dangerous, too."

The Fixer made a disparaging sound. The man's pride was as enormous as his ego.

"But wasn't Rafe your pal, too?" Josh said, putting his best chef-describing-his-favorite-recipe amiable voice. "And wouldn't the Don give some mark of appreciation to the one special man who solved the murder of his favorite nephew?"

The car went quiet, only the humming of the hybrid motor filling the cabin. Then a burst of laughter shattered the silence, in the weird hiccupping way of someone who rarely gave into the impulse.

"That old rascal has definitely tainted you, wild boy," the Fixer said. "'Cause you sure inherited his silver tongue!"

49 - A SATISFIED CLIENT

I RECOMMEND THE SOLE, TODAY," Rob said to his favorite pair of lovers.

Mrs. Porter wore a light blue knitted sweater with a white dove on the breast, and a wide-rimmed whey hat, obviously from one of the shops. She looked totally hot, or, rather, cool under it.

Her bespectacled eyes went to the new Kon-Tiki picture on the wall.

"So happy you got it back," she said. "It adds to the spirit of the place."

Drama or no drama, they had opened the restaurant the day after their return from The City That Never Slept, one week ago.

Rob had been sent to purchase new glasses, and liquors. (He was mightily annoyed to be asked his ID card for the alcohol.) All this using "pocket money" from the Family. True to their word, they had not harassed Josh's parents, who had promised to visit by the end of the summer.

And Josh was beaming at not having to hide himself

anymore. His bar had returned to his former splendor and was popular in the evenings. He was envisioning making a down payment towards a house, instead of his flat. Rob himself was not adverse to putting out roots in this community and, maybe, some day, reach out to his parents. For now, Mel had come twice to help out in the evenings. This way, they returned to their flat together.

All in all, Rob had drifted closer to Josh, and the nice weather was bringing more clients to their terrace. He had gotten used to the regulars, like the Porters, Meave and Stan. And some occasional, like the graying mayor who stopped for a quick coffee, the baby-carrying woman who stopped for a glass of fizzy water, and the ice cream shack lady, whom Josh cavalierly called Vera.

Last time, Josh had greeted her with a good-natured "Testing the concurrence, Vera?"

To which she had replied on the same carefree tone, pushing up her pink round sunglasses that gave her an insectoid appearance.

"Someone said once that you could live on ice cream alone, but I don't want to test that theory."

But now, Vera would be at the shack, distributing calories.

Mrs. Porter was squinting, looking at Josh.

"Don't you think your patron has changed?" she asked.

The elderly lady, being observant, remarked on the light fuzz now forming on Josh's head, obscuring some of the ink.

"Oh, he's not a fan of getting sunburn," Rob said, smiling at the charming couple.

He felt better. It had taken the week to reel off the high cliff Josh and Rob had almost plunged from.

TRUE TO THEIR HABIT, the Porters were enthralled by their meal. They left more satiated, Mr. Porter lifting his cane in a salute to the chef.

Rob was taking up the empty plates when he noticed a new client making his way up the steps. His sense of feeling better melted like ice cream left on the counter.

The man's thick black hair were covered by a baseball cap and a polo that looked expensive with the small crocodile on it, and his eyes obscured by more expensive sunglasses. However, Rob recognized the snarky lines around the mouth.

The Fixer rose his eyes, and plopped down at one empty table with a thick slab-like menu.

"What would you recommend, miracle boy?" he said.

JOSH WAS FINISHING a finicky *roux* when his elf bounced inside the kitchen area.

"He's here," he said.

Henry put his head out of the Thermidor's oven, where he had been checking the failing back LED light.

"Who's he?" he said.

But Josh knew there was only one *he* that could send his fiery waiter in this state of giddiness.

"Take his order," he said to Rob. "I'm coming."

He hurried to beat the sauce into a satisfying pulp, then gave it to Henry for the finishing touches. He could not delay this meeting anymore, however unsavory this character was.

He lumbered out on the sunny terrace. Had it been

only last week since he had discovered the act of vandalism? There were currently four clients enjoying the *mets du jour* and two young women were looking at the menu nailed to the post.

The Fixer had diverted him self from his dark mean suit. He wore a pair of chino pants and a Lacoste polo shirt that Rafe would not have spurned. He had wisely chosen a wide-brimmed cap obviously bought at the first souvenir shop of the pier.

Rob was suggesting the turbot plate in white sauce and parsley, but his eye was gliding to the women consulting the menu a few feet from them.

The Fixer's eye lit up as Josh made his way to the table.

"I don't have a lot of time," he said.

The mobster shrug, gave the menu back to Rob.

"I'll get your day plate, Wonder boy," he said.

Josh did not care for the fancy surnames the Fixer had found for Rob, but it beat the more insulting ones he had used at the abandoned cannery plant. He pointed with his chin to the women chatting at the menu, and Rob strode to them.

"Ha, take a break, wild boy," the Fixer said.

He fished out a newspaper from his pocket and spread it on the surface. It was a Washington Post, the previous day edition. A fiftyish-man was grinning from the front page. The header over it told: *Cold case solved; A senator arrested for mobster's murder*.

"So you found him?" Josh asked.

The Fixer looked around them. The clients were engrossed into the conversation.

"Just read on," he said.

Josh understood the need for discretion, and sat. The man slid the newspaper across the table. He could hear

Rob's spoking to the ladies about the plat du jour that Henry was wrestling from the Thermidor.

As he read, a lot of Rafe's cryptic declarations made sense. The "fish" he had thought to reel in had been a bull-headed politician who had sustained staggering losses at a casino and that Rafe had gallantly (*or not so gallantly*, Josh though) rescued by lending enough credit to pay back the casino.

Rafe had gotten his hooks on the man, threatening to reveal the politician's losses, and his womanizing, shameful for a bible-thumping senator. He knew the man had resources, so he had sent Josh on a business trip to make sure he wouldn't be around. He had though Rafe had met his killer at the restaurant, but the truth, as leaked by the Fixer, had been uglier.

Rafe had been shot and killed in the empty an alley behind a shady strip joint, by the politician's cronies. Rafe's body had been moved in the wee hours of the night to the Lucky Traveler's basement, using the dead man's key to elude the system alarm.

Then they set fire to the place.

"How did you find who did it?"

"Just had to follow the paper trail of the casinos, dig deep, to find the name of the guy our nice Rafe had helped out of his debts."

"You did all that legwork?"

The Fixer pulled the rim of his hat over his brow, shading his eyes.

"Remember, he was my pal, too. So I pulled all stops to dig up the cronies who had done his bidding."

"Did the man confess?" Josh asked, his voice thick. "If he wasn't onsite..."

"*Ya* bet he did not soil his hands! But once I applied the

right incentive on the cronies (*he brushed his index and thumb in the universal sign*), they were more than happy to blab on him. The good senator sang as a bird once he got nabbed."

Josh knew not to ask details in public; the Fixer brought a thick paper envelope out of his breast pocket.

"Before the cops burst in his clean house, I paid a little visit to him. Just had to lean on him with the truth, to make him part with this small bundle. The Don thinks I could keep half and give half to you."

Josh fingered the brown envelope, weighting the banknotes inside.

"This is clean money, no strings attached. Cash contributions to the great man's campaign. You've earned it."

Josh slid the envelope in his apron as Rob brought the plate. The lemon and almond sauce, mixed with herbs, floated up, adding to the fish's crisp skin. The Fixer did not hide his olfactive pleasure.

"I must say, you're quite the cook, wild boy," he said.

To which Josh replied.

"And I must admit you're quite the detective."

Josh wondered how he dared smile at the sharkish mobster, but he guessed his dear Rafe would have been happy to know his murder had been solved.

50 - THE PIER

THE NEXT DAY was a pouting Saturday, with the sun hiding behind clouds. Rob searched for his handicapped gull, but did not find the bird. He tried not to think about the realities of life, when things were finally looking up for Josh and him.

Henry was not in, yet, so Rob bent under the Thermidor's base. A thin layer of dust lay undisturbed, except where Josh's fingers had pushed the brown envelope under. It was a dark mass, like a wooden plank, and you had to know it was there to see it.

Nevertheless, he hoped the thing would find its way into a bank account soon.

Last night, after closing the place, Josh had shown him the envelope. It was heavy enough, and the banknotes packed inside had smelled like mold.

It had been too late for the banks, and his boss did not trust the automated tellers, nor did he trust going to an automated teller in a Friday night full of drunken revelers. Because he did not trust the dinked little safe under the bar, either, Josh had hidden the cash under the vast Thermidor's base, to retrieve later.

~

THE SUN HAD COME out of the gray mattress of clouds when the Kon Tikki opened, at its appointed time. Henry was busy with the Thermidor firing from all rounds in blue flames, so Josh would wait for an occasion to pull out the packet without the cook noticing.

But the animation of the harbor and the bustle of clients got all their attention, one couple claiming the sun hurt their eyes, Josh adjusting the parasol, then this other client changing his mind after looking up the prices, leaving Rob to zoom in the kitchen warn the cook to not begin the frying. This just before he popped out, to find an anxious lady announcing she was on a keto diet and would they have a fiber less meal please?

All in all, not a bad day, with clients paying in plastic negating the need for the little safe.

As he was chasing birds away from the generous left over abandoned by the keto-lady, Rob noticed the closed-cropped head of Maeve. The young woman was heading for the pier's end, where she could watch her cute fisherman without being see. Rob smiled: she was so transparent!

At last, he had finished cleaning the tables and putting the wrapped utensils for the next batch of guests. This would be the time when he had learned to expect the Porters to come in. He had seen them going down the pier earlier.

~

Henry was still growling at the Thermidor, and Josh was entreating him to be patient, when Rob left for a brief bathroom break.

For the creature comforts, most of the shops relied on a row of three portable units on the side of the little coffee place. Even wrapped in a cedar wardrobe and often fumigated, their function was obvious.

Getting out, Rob leaned over the railing, to fill his eyes with the calm beauty of the sea.

That's when a loud cawing erupted over his head.

Now, now, now!

He looked up, and smiled at the one-legged gull.

"Hey, Goalie, I really thought you were out for the count," he said.

He expected his bird to settle on a post and hope for tidbits. But no, Goalie kept flapping up and harking, in an almost comical fashion.

"OK, OK, you 'think I'm skirting work? What are you, my conscience?'"

Rob flapped his own arms to scare it. The gull flew, cawing and spitting, down the pier.

Then Rob became aware of a pop of pressure in his ears, like in a plane as it climbed altitude. He heard another gull, nothing irregular there, but then, it seemed like the harking and cawing had multiplied.

The lady at the serving window of the ice cream shack craned her neck to peer out, squinting.

Rob felt like in a weird Disney movie: everywhere, on the railing posts, on the loo's roofs, on the garbage bins, on the boats masts, hundreds of gulls took to the sky in one common cry, leaping up from their chosen perch. Ignoring the food scraps they were disputing, they flew up.

The birds were not the only ones making noise. Rob

heard the high-pitched yelp of a small dog. The lower whimpering of a golden retriever trailing a tourist farther away joined. Even the house sparrows stealing crumbs tweeted high and low, more agitated than usual.

Many passerby, among whom he spotted his favorite couple of old lovers, had stopped and were peering at the confused cloud of white bodies, with a smattering of darker cormorants.

Then he felt a trembling under his legs. The deck was thrumming, as if a heavy truck was running its engine. By reflex, Rob grabbed the railing. A new sound was filling his ears, the low rumble of a very large animal.

That's when he noticed the walls of the ice cream parlor, swaying. The lady at the window emitted a surprised *eep!* and disappeared.

Beyond his position at the end of the pier, all the white boats on the docks were swaying, too, as large smelly waves smashed against their pristine hulls.

The rumble rose along with the smell of dead things, from the waves, from the wooden deck itself. Some people who had been walking off the ice cream shack lost their balance and fell, either dropping their unfinished cone or their half-opened wallet, crying in dismay.

Belatedly, Rob's sluggish brain made the connection.

A quake!

51 - EARTHQUAKE

A SECOND LATER, the deafening crack of something big breaking echoed in the air.

The floorboards were sliding under his feet. A scent of vanilla ice cream pervaded the air, mixing with a dank smell of the flotsam.

"Mister, can you help?" A harried voice called.

The ice cream shack lady – Vera Something- was back at her window. He pivoted on his feet, to see her taking down her sugar-stained apron.

"The back door's stuck," she said, placing her gloved hands on the sill. "I have to get through this window."

The exit was not large, and a man like Josh would never slip though it. But Vera was a smallish woman. She heaved her upper body up, her arms ramrod straight, pushing, until her hips caught the aluminum frame of the window.

Rob instantly saw the window would be too narrow, but he grabbed her under the arms.

"Let go," he said. "I'll pull you out."

He used all his wiry might to twist Vera's shoulders to

turn her hips in a diagonal position. The he pulled. Inch by inch, the woman's khaki pants cleared the window. She flopped down with him, winded.

A puffy *thanks, thanks!* blew off her lips as she plunked her spectacles on the bridge of her nose.

Rob helped her to her feet and led her on the promenade, toward the land. By then, the tremors had ended, but horrid sounds from the unseen breaking things continued.

A flow of vividly dressed clients poured from the shops.

He got a glimpse of Josh's head over the flow. The crowd parted for a moment to give Rob a glimpse of the nice Porters who had not chosen the right time to stop by. The wife was clutching at the folds of her husband's windbreaker and Josh's meaty arm. The husband was clutching at his wife's hand and his cane.

Henry's rotund figure in white was getting out, too.

Then the deck tilted, sideways, a few degrees at first, which made the young children laugh until the mother scooped them up. Then deck lurched in a sudden slump, the railing breaking in places, sending one Bermuda-clad tourist overboard.

Rob barely had the time to notice the man's head bobbing up, as he regained his balance.

The tilting of the deck convinced the reticent tourists who had hoped to wait out the seism to scamper. The seism might not have been high on the Richter scale, but the pier had somehow been impacted, some hidden struts given way.

He couldn't see Josh any more, as the hundreds of persons were crowding the promenade. Then, a new idea crowded his mind as he passed the steps leading to the Kon Tikki terrace.

Rob let go of Vera.

"You can make it to the land?" he asked.

She nodded.

"Your next cone's on the house," she said.

Rob turned back, on the swaying planks, as the coffee shop clients were staggering forward.

He was about to heave himself on the terrace, when another thick, moist crack echoed, and the whole seaward half of the pier flipped on its side, projecting the hapless people still fleeing in the water. Rob grabbed the bamboo posts.

The tables and chairs slid down, along with the cutlery. The furniture was stopped by the terrace railing, but all smaller elements, cutlery, glasses, napkins, slab-style menus, passed like through a big sieve, slid through the width of the promenade, and plunged in the foaming waves.

The sea had reacted to the quake, the normally blue-green waters tuning an ugly brown, obscured by all the sediments. Images of the 2004 tsunami had imprinted in Rob's mind. He looked to the horizon: no dark line profiled itself. But dismayed screams were rising from the beach, assaulted by gurgling waves.

The people there were getting up in haste as the edge of a brown, foaming wave reached up, and up to their gaudy colored towels. Grabbing their children or loved ones, the beach goers retreated over the sloping rock, or ran to the parking lot adjacent to the end of Ocean View street.

But the railings and structures, and water ducts were still anchored together, and to the land. So the deck undulated like a angry snake, the floorboards cracking under the tension, exhaling the moist dead weed odor of the support beams.

And the shops were swaying like slow-motion drunkards… The corrugated roofs were straining against the screw that held it to the 2x4 section beams, with almost cinematographic screeches.

Rob was now climbing the terrace, inclined at forty degrees. He grabbed the bar counter and pulled himself up, grateful the whole bar had been riveted in place by the previous administration.

He ascended through the kitchen entrance, his fingers finding a brief purchase in the door's white frame. As he pushed himself inside, he was shocked by the chaotic state of the kitchen. The chairs, tabourets and tables had tumbled against the wall in a heap of thin metal legs. Gravity had pulled open the counter drawers, the stainless steel utensils clamoring to get out.

The tall refrigerator at the back wall near the window was leaning dangerously forward. As for the Thermidor… Henry had shut of the gas adduction, bless his dear old heart. But the massive silver oven was trying to escape, too, helped by the incline, with only the thick electrical chord keeping it in check. The other appliances were dancing as well. The sole stable element was the industrial-sized steel sink and the range hood over the Thermidor.

He moved on all four under the working table, feeling the tenuous surface of the plywood floor.

He grabbed the sink's copper ducts. He couldn't see if the envelope was still under the range. He perched himself up, both feet in the sink. That's when he saw the well-padded envelope, sliding under the taut electrical chord.

The money that Josh had forgotten, in his haste to get his clients to safety.

A roar of splinted timbers and frantic cries from both gulls and humans filled the air. He had thought the tremors gone, but the floor was heaving under him, and more water was rushing to fill the kitchen.

The pier that had been the pride of Safe Harbor was sinking! He had to grab the money. Before… The soaked plywood panels of the floor, no longer supported by the beams, were now more than 50 percent incline.

The Atlantic was inviting itself in the kitchen, having gobbled the terrace under its turbid, opaque mass. Only half the height of the door remained clear of the dark soup pouring in. Many things floated besides the yellow bulbs of jellyfishes, pizza boxes and plastic bottles and white polyethylene coffee cups and plastic spoons…

The overhead lights that so facilitate the cooking, petered out. The refrigerator fell silent, which was a shock. Its droning hum had been the constant background noise under the clatter of utensils in the kitchen.

The electrical line had been cut. Fortunately, day light filtered by the door and the rear window.

If he found the envelope, he would have to dive in those murky waters to get out.

He kneeled in the sink, using the sides to prop him erect, and lowered one arm, sweeping the floor under the line. His fingers brushed the envelope.

That was sliding now, following the sharper incline.

C. A.!

He changed position, grabbing the metal sink with one hand, and stomped on a corner of the envelope, as the water was reaching it. Its content was too heavy to float.

He managed to pick it up, and retreated in the sink. His pants were drenched, his balance compromised by the weird angles of everything.

The loud ring of copper ducts hitting each other and

the sloshing of water against metal appliances surfaces was multiplied as the volume in the kitchen dwindled.

He swam to the cupboard, keeping the envelope free of the dark soup. His mother would have told him how stupid it was to risk his life for a wad of cash. But that money could help a lot of people, especially to repair the damages.

The enclosed air was charged with miasmas, dead seaweeds, and medusa stink like plastic toys covered with mold. Empty plastic bottles bobbed along with the glossy red slab-style menus.

Then, the range's power cords snapped entirely. The Thermidor initiated its ponderous slide to crash against the front wall. By now, only the front door upper sill was visible. Rob had seen war movies with sinking ships, but never had he thought he would star in one.

Or die in one.

He guessed the other shops had undergone similar damages. The Kon Tikki's corrugated roof screeched again, as the steel panels glided against each other, only kept in place by screws.

He had to get out of the death trap. The back window could let him out, but would he reach it?

He heard the loud call of Goalie, from the roof.

Now-now-now!

52 - NIGHTMARE

Josh was living a nightmare.

First, as he was greeting his favorite clients, the damn gulls had started a wild party overhead, coasting in ever-widening circles.

And not just the gulls, but all the other flying pests: the brown sparrows, the black cormorants rising from the sea itself, all leaving the ground without order.

Then the dogs had started yapping out, and this was when Josh knew, seconds before he felt a vibration under his feet, and heard the tinkle of the glasses and bottles jumping in the bar enclosure, and the empty chairs legs tapping against the floor boards of the terrace. Under those superficial sounds, rolled the deep breath of a vast organism usually ignored by humans, made of land and sea together.

Josh had lived through one major earthquake before, a long time ago, so he reacted before most of the tourists. His grandfather had told young Joshua what to do, and the most important instruction.

"Get out! Out! Everyone's out!" he called out, prodding his patrons to vacate the tables, waving toward the land.

"Why? It just an earthquake," one guy seated at the bar said, nursing his drink.

That's when a loud, moist cracks sounded.

"OUT!"

As he was shouting his lungs off, all the joints and beams of the terraces groaned under the strain.

He tensed. New-Zealand was located dead on the fault between the Pacific and Indo-Australian plates, and subject to more than its share of devastating quakes. But here, in the more stable Maine coast?

No time to study the problem: Josh grabbed the reticent bar patron and spurred him on. He directed the others to the foot of the pier, lamenting the beautiful plates Henry had painstakingly prepared and that Josh, as chef, had decorated.

Henry.

Josh put his head inside the kitchen door, seeing the cook juggling with his pots and pans, the steam of boiling water escaping from the main pot blurring his face.

"Henry! Rob! Leave it!"

The cook's head whipped, alarmed by Josh's urgent tone.

"What's up, boss?" he said.

But Josh was already inside the kitchen, closing all gas stovetops, grasping the cook's fleshy arm, pulling him out of the death trap that the pier would become if a tsunami crashed on it. He didn't see Rob.

"Where's Rob?" He asked.

"Aw, gone to the loos, I think, or giving snippets to his half assed bird."

As he pulled the cook outside, Josh heard a series of

low-pitch thumps echoed, as if a giant was walking on the pier. They culminated on a loud crack, coming from everywhere.

"What in the sweet…" Henry began, but he couldn't finish.

The promenade deck tilted, sideways, like the bridge of a rolling ship. In an instant, Josh understood that half of the posts supporting the pier had collapsed, leaving the other half under an increase strain.

He saw the Porters struggling to hold to the bamboo beams framing the terrace. Maeve the pixie girl was there, too, helping them.

Screams erupted from the other souvenir shops and restaurants and coffees, and clients poured out like blood cells from a ruptured artery. He had no time to search for his elf. Focus. He grabbed the frail woman's arm as Maeve helped on the other side.

Under a tempest of bird cries, the foursome of them progressed, leaning on the railing that he hoped would hold. Greasy, murky water lapped at their feet as the deck slid more and more.

Dark, algae-smelling water sloshed at their feet as Josh negotiated the slanted deck. He held the right arm of Mr. Porter, leaning on his cane, and gripped the left hand of his whispery haired wife, braced against the life-saving railing.

The slippery boards under the layer of flotsam forced him to slow down. Maeve lips were taut, as if she knew the danger, and only parted to give an encouragement to the old couple.

He ignored the crunch of glass and refuse under his soles as he lugged the Porters forward, ignored the rumble of more structural damage occurring in his back, of dozens of cellphones clamoring in every ringtone possible around them (including a very confusing guy's voice saying *whassuuup?*) intent on only one thing: getting his clients to the upper ground.

Relief filled Josh when he felt hard concrete under his shoes. They had reached the transition between the wooden deck of the promenade and the asphalted parking lot. Josh kept close to the (intact) wall of the souvenir shop at the end of the parking, resting on a big pad of concrete.

To his relief, he saw that firefighters and other orange-vest wearing rescuers were about, directing the milling crowd toward the strip of beach. Lots of people, who hadn't been on the pier, were out and excited and curious, holding the cams high over their head.

Heavy steps pounded the deck and a wide-shouldered firefighter extended a hand to help up Mrs. Porter.

"This way ma'am, please," the firefighter said, pointing to the beach, that was filling by the minute with more people.

"Ray?" she called.

Mr. Porter stomped the end of his cane on the concrete, with the verve of an explorer taking possession of the territories.

"Ha!" he said with a hint of pride. "I've seen worse!"

Then, he followed his wife, with the big firefighter dwarfing them. The man had a calm, clear voice, used to reassure frightened people.

His black jeans dripping with water, Josh was reeling from the suddenness, the stress, and the danger. He felt as if he had just ran a marathon, to get the frail couple to safety.

The he turned, and discovered what had happened in his back.

The beams and struts of the pier peeking off the water like giant, blackened toothpicks. There was nothing left of the promenade, except a few slanted roofs and the big ice cream cone, the rest of the façade invisible.

The marina dock beside the pier was partially visible: the capsized yachts, the white-hulled sailboats masts leaning haphazardly, like drunken sailors. The horizon was a blurred line, despite the sun shining without shame.

He could see a part of the Kon Tikki's corrugated roof jutting of the water, and a stupid gull flapping his wings there as if the bird was the new king of the place. More seabirds were drifting in the sky, maybe surprised their favorite perching spot had been destroyed.

Destroyed, also, all the pricey appliances he had invested in. His beautiful terrace adorned with bamboo was under water. He couldn't see the back wall from his position, but, the steep angle of the roof told him the kitchen was drowned, with only the top of the fridge emerging. If the big metal box had stayed in place.

Josh bit his lower lip, closing his eyes to shut off the public, the excited or angry murmurs, the drumming clicks of cell phones taking pictures.

After all he's done to save his restaurant, and his reputation, and his life, a stupid earthquake had thrown his business to the ground. Or, rather, to the sea.

"I, I am so sorry for your place," a voice said behind him.

He came back to himself in a rush.

A tall gray-haired woman was looking at him, her eyes level with his. Her features were arranged in the distraught expression of someone arriving on a disaster area, her green cell phone in one hand, a paper bag smelling of warm oats muffins. Josh recognized the Green Crusader.

He was about to express a platitude, when his hands went to the pouch hanging in the front of his apron, tickling with small change. His eyes went wide.

With all the people to get to safety, he had forgotten the Fixer's little gift.

"What?" she said.

"The cash-register," he said to cover the truth. "I forgot to empty it yesterday."

Her gray eyes blinked in sympathy.

"Was there a lot in it?"

Josh sighed, then regained his own composure. The Green Crusader had her own problems.

"It just cash," he said. "Humans are more important."

He scanned the flow of people going up the main street.

"But I would like to make sure my new waiter is OK."

However, her expression changed, as if Josh's own worry had been contagious.

"Maeve!" Kathleen said, suddenly. "Have you seen her? She was on the pier…"

"Oh, yes," Josh said, "she was just her with me, here…"

He stopped. The young woman had been a step behind him, helping him bring the Porters, and then...

"She, she went back there," he said.

Josh recognized the yellow manes floating, sloshing in a soggy heap. The storm had pushed them to the shore. The shore that was filling, both with jellyfishes, dead fishes, and drenched people.

"Please, step back," a policemen said, unrolling a bundle of bright orange plastic around the perimeter of the parking lot.

Josh felt faint: as he saw again the charred ruins of his

restaurant, the yellow crime scene tape with the words DANGER DO NOT CROSS repeating themselves ad nauseam.

"Maybe they're on the beach," the hard-faced woman said.

He looked, a hope in his face.

"Yes, maybe he went there," he said.

She cleaved her way through the onlookers, with the ease of a long practice. Josh followed her, his toes sloshing in his running shoes as he thread the sidewalk to the beach. The rumble of many voices formed a background on the beach, cut by orders from an authoritative voices directing the foot traffic.

53 - OLD MAN'S ROCK

THE LOWER PART of the beach had been swept under a black wave of sea and human refuse, forcing most onlookers over the big rock, or the upped slope of the beach where the vegetation battled to stabilize the sand aground.

The tall woman groaned. Josh followed her gaze.

Shoots of willow and aspen formed a green advancing army on the upper beach, their roots stabilizing the nomadic sand grains, until it met the concrete edge of the street and the parking lot. Most of those sprouts were now broken under a crowd of unwary feet.

Josh walked among the crowd in search of Rob. Kathleen met the young ripped guy, Alan and his friend Louise, both ragged and drenched. They had helped some of the sea-thrown people get to the shore. Locals were bringing coverlets to the drenched victims.

Kathleen stopped to make a call.

Josh had tried to call Rob, and got the automated company message. His elf had either not come with his phone or the phone had discharged. Or... He stomped his foot in the moist sand. He was not ready to consider the other possibilities.

Josh looked up, at the Old Man's rock face. A few people had climbed the rock to get a better view. No Rob among them.

He climbed on the inclined surface, the crevices and imitated them, and pivoted slowly, to scan the beach area.

"Did you find him?"

He jumped, then relaxed as he recognized Kathleen, minus her pastry bag. He surmised she had made her distribution.

"No," he said. "Rob's not here. And he's not responding to my calls."

The corners of his mouth were taut with apprehension.

"I'm afraid he…"

Josh did not finish. Couldn't finish this sentence, like a death sentence. He sat down abruptly on the rock.

"Shit, oh shit," he groaned, hugging his knees. "Not again…"

He was trembling all over, as if his body couldn't contain the reality of losing Rob. Identifying the body. Attending the funerals. Going on without his elf. He buried his face in his arms.

The sunbaked rock under him reminded him of all the days perched on a jutting rock with his grandad, as they looked out at the sun emerging from the sea. He missed the old man so much. He would give anything to be a small boy again, his grandfather towering over him, a benevolent tower.

He heard a rustle of fabric beside him. He opened his eyes. Kathleen, her soft gray eyes on him. She stood, silent, not seeing, or not judging, his tears.

"Let's look together," she said. "We're better placed here."

Josh got up, his joints crying. Kathleen had shaded her eyes and was slowly revolving around her axe, looking out. Likewise, he searched the horizon, from the north arc to the south.

The waves were glinting in the mocking sun, as he looked for a mop of red hair.

By now, most of the people who had fallen from the pier had been rescued, thanks to the shallow water. But those who had been at the end of the pier, close to the ice cream shack, would have been deported in the stronger current moving volumes of sea water to the north.

Josh cringed inside, because Rob had revealed he was not a very good swimmer…

At this distance, more than a kilometer from the pier, all people were dots, tiny dots. Yellow and orange dots, the volunteers and firemen, moved along the wreckage. Black dotes, the police. White dot, the doctor's white coat. Two black dots bouncing up and down in a yellow inflatable boat.

He let his eyes roam the waters. He had a good sight, but the endless incoming waves, their crests and hollows, mocked him. *Where are you, damn elf?* he thought.

A bright red flash blinked between two white-tipped crests.

"What's that?" Josh said.

As he spoke, the scarlet flash teased his eyes again.

Kathleen turned to him, questing.

"What did you see?" she asked.

"Something flashed, there. Red."

He pointed one arm toward the white-tipped waves.

The sunrays were playing on the foamy tips, reflecting a blinding light.

Then, he saw it, again, the scarlet red flash, tracing a circle in the air. Before a wave hid it. It had been a bright red…

"It's one of my menus!" Josh said, his voice croaking.

Kathleen gaped at him.

"Those big rigid things with the giant lobsters?"

"Someone's holding the menu up!"

"Rob?" Kathleen asked.

Josh squinted his best, discarding all distracting elements: foam tips, whooshing noise, gulls swooping by… But the flash was shrinking, carried to the large by the swift current.

"Can't see for sure," he said finally.

Besides him, Kathleen had seized her cell, punched keys. By now, she was speaking to someone in charge. He heard only part of the hurried conversation, as he searched for the red flash.

"…about one mile deep," she was saying. "You must help him!"

There was an answer that raised a dispirited gasp form the hard faced woman. Of course, rescue teams would be busy. But she hissed, and push keys on her old thing.

She waited, her face tense, then let out a relieved sigh as a tinny voice answered her.

"Stan! Where are you?"

Her fisherman nephew was answering. Where was he? Josh would have seen that unmistakable blue boat.

"A young man is adrift in the current," she was saying. "He'll drown if you don't find him."

She talked some more, before closing up the thing. By now, Josh had noticed the red flash drifting away. The currents were stronger. He scanned again, his hands shading his eyes.

Nothing. The crests of the waves were too high.

Kathleen expelled a burst of air besides him. He followed her gaze, to the gray line of concrete wave breakers and the small tower. Suddenly, a blue hull passed behind the white lighthouse, its prow cleaving the waters, in a foamy V.

As it passed the damaged pier, the boat slowed down. Josh wished the fisherman to go faster, because Rob would get farther, but it made sense: Stan could pass over a swimmer with his boat.

So the blue hull proceeded at low speed, turning to the north and following the direction of the main current.

He got a glimpse of the red flash, again.

Hold on, Rob, he thought. *Please, hold down.*

54 - BREAKING UP INSIDE

JOSH FOLLOWED the progress of the blue boat, with the name painted in golden letters. Stanley was invisible, inside the boxy cabin. The blue hull dipped over and under the crests, leaving its own white disturbance.

Somehow, Rob had taken hold of a floating timber, the dark cylinder peeking off a rare crest, along with the menu.

Then, Josh didn't see anything. Both timber and Rob were too remote. The blue boat had swerved toward the horizon. The engine had stopped producing

The waves partially hid the rescue, but suddenly there were one bluish smudge on stern, then, after another dip in the hollow of a green wave, there were two smudges, one big one small.

"Who is it?" He asked.

Well, there was a way to know.

Kathleen pulled out her phone and called again.

There was a long pause. Josh heard the tinny male voice at the other end. Interrogative. But he couldn't miss the happy pitch in the voice.

"Who's with you?" Kathleen asked.

Josh didn't get the answer. But Kathleen's face beamed up with relief. Then her pale eyes went cloudy as she looked at him.

"It's Maeve," she said, after hanging up.

Josh felt himself breaking up inside. But he forced himself to smile. He knew the pixie-like young woman, how easy it had been to talk with her. He knew Rob had a high opinion of her. He couldn't be *that* egoist?

"I'm, I'm happy for her," he said, his voice lacking substance.

Then, he let his head dip. He stood there, forlorn.

A veined hand touched his forearm.

"Look," Kathleen said. "Maybe Rob is among the wounded in the parking."

He turned to her expectant face, noticing the gray strands escaping her off-white hat. The activity on the quaint beach parking had ballooned: many cars were gone, and instead, ambulances were advancing and retreating. A man in white coat – the wiry doctor who treated him, asking less than nothing – was ambling along, bending on the reclining forms.

"There's only one way to know," she said in this firm mom-knows-best voice. "Go there and ask."

He let out a skeptical groan.

"Like asking for directions," he said. "I'm not very good at it."

Kathleen's mouth twisted in a smirk, as if she were remembering a personal joke. Then it was gone, and her expression returned to pensive.

"Then, let's go together and ask," she said, taking his arm.

Josh let her guide him down the sloping surface,

refusing to look past the tips of his shoes. He would get an answer soon enough. For now, he focused on the veins of pale quartz and darker volcanic rock crossing the pale rock under his feet.

WHEN THEY REACHED the sandy area of the beach, he became aware of many people standing there or talking, or staring at him. But Kathleen's firm hand pulled Josh through, and he felt like a child again, guided by his granddad.

Then, his running shoes hit the concrete pavement of the parking.

People lay on the ground, or sat on folding chairs brought by helpful neighbors or shop keepers, one arm in a scarf. Josh had seen war movies with improvised hospital wards full of wounded, moaning and groaning in pain. The parking looked like it, at a smaller scale.

What was not in the movie were the smells of blood and urine that rose from the parking lot. His stomach clenched in a tight ball. There were less of the wounded now, because ambulances had come and were whisking the worst cases away, but enough remained to give him the impression of a dispensary in those war movies.

As he was looking on, he felt his heart drop. His hand squeezed the tall woman's hand, by reflex, like a child.

The collapse had made casualties.

The wiry doctor was pulling a long, dark plastic shroud over a body. He got up and gave a string of instructions to a dark-skinned woman and a too-pale emergency tech. His dark eyes caught them approaching.

257

"Kathleen, I'm so sorry," he said. "I couldn't do anything…"

His voice had almost reverted to a child's. Kathleen gave him a quick, one-armed hug.

"You're doing your best, Zee," she said.

Josh had been right: there was some current between the two of them. Like between him and Rob. His eyes latched onto the length of the plastic shroud: adult-sized. Thin body.

He sucked in a breath of moisture laden air. *Rafe's bodybag would have been this size*, he thought.

The the hard-faced woman squeezed his hand. She addressed the doctor.

"Ziad, this is Josh Tallgate."

The doctor's eyes lifted up to Josh's dragon-tattooed mass.

"Oh, I know you, the Kon Tikki manager."

"Yes," Kathleen said. "He is seeking his employee. You remember, young Rob… was he among the wounded?"

The doctor blinked.

"What he's like?"

Josh answered, he could not detach his gaze from the Rob-shaped shroud.

"Thin, mid-height, hair like orange flames…" he began, then his throat locked his voice in.

He was barely aware of the tears streaming on his cheeks as he stepped closer to the bag. Until the point of his running shoes almost touched the dark plastic. He did not want to know, because not knowing the identity of the deceased lying down kept his Rob alive.

Then, he let go of Kathleen's hand to touch the plastic tarp. Brown fingers closed on his tattooed wrist.

"Don't," the doctor's voice said.

Josh's head swiveled in his direction.

"It's a brown-haired man," The man said, in a low voice. "Head crushed. Nothing I could do."

Josh emitted a strangled sound. Shivers ran through his body. The negative answer did nothing to alleviate his concerns. An ambulance drew near the thin doctor, one emergency tech asked for instructions. A gurney was produced.

Again, the tall woman wound her thin arm through Josh's.

"Let's go," she said.

Her face was scrunched in her own anger, and Josh could hear the china-like grinding of her teeth. He remembered the pics she had shown him. He could guess she was stymied by this situation, brought up by the neglect rotting under the pier.

55 - GULL'S CALL

Josh moved like an automaton, no knowing where to go. He scanned the crowd, again, without finding his friend's red flame. The doctor's negative answer had not discarded his gnawing worry. He averted his eyes from the ruins of the Kon Tikki, from the yellow dinghies coming to shore.

Rob could be drifting under those waves, invisible. The undertow would whisk him away. His grandfather had explained to Josh how the sea could carry the bodies over long distances.

The raucous *Now, now, now!* of gulls circling overhead roused him. Was it Rob's one-leg bird? He stared at the ocean, squinting as the sun plunged through the layers of clouds promising new rain for the next days.

The sound of angry voices penetrated his concentration. A barkeeps reflex, he came instantly aware of something odd.

Not because of the altercation *per se* ("Who are you, the girlfriend?" a man asked in a grating voice), but because he recognized the young woman's high-pitched voice, answering to some troopers. Her back was turned to him, as she was gesturing to a burly State trooper holding a familiar flour bin.

"I am a patron of the Kon Tikki restaurant…," the pixie-like Maeve was saying.

Josh was surprised by this authoritative, confident tone he had never heard from the small woman at his restaurant. So it took him a short processing delay to sort out the others on the scene.

Behind the burly trooper, another uniformed man was holding the arm of a dripping-clothed tourist, only the pale, sea-weed decorated arm being visible, since the two men of law were positioned between Josh and him.

But the arm held had some seaweed on the skin. No, it was a wave pattern Josh had beheld, and kissed several times…

Maeve's voice rose, imperative, the kind that you couldn't ignore, each syllable neat and precise rising over the din of many conversations.

"And I can *bear witness* that Rob here…"

A new sun lit up inside Josh as he saw the magical being, now un-eclipsed by the burly troopers, standing close to the short-cropped Maeve.

"…is a *diligent, honest* and fantastic…"

Josh's brain flipped. His body acted by itself before the young woman finished her declaration. A cry of mingled anguish and relief erupted from his throat as he pounded the pavement.

"ROB!"

The young woman stepped aside. Rob had barely the time to look up before Josh' arms bore on him.

Rob was alive, even if soaking wet.

He lifted the slender redhead in a bear embrace, feeling the water squish from the damped server's outfit, drops splashing in a circle around them. How long had it been since he had felt this lightness?

"You son of a gun!" Josh said, half-crying, half-laughing. "Where were you? I searched everywhere! I though you were…"

He expelled a rush of air from his throat.

Rob had wrapped himself around Josh's waist, legs and arms locked. Josh felt fortunate his ribs had manded, because the tight leg embrace would have broken them again. He felt Rob's panting against his shoulder, words tumbling off his lips.

"There, see, I was out to the john, then the pier shook, and the ice cream lady needed to get out, and I saw you getting the people out…"

Josh barely understood the flow of hurried words, only conscious of the slender elf's body, his clothes sodden and smelly, but safe, safe against him.

"And, and, of course, you wouldn't have taken the stash!"

Josh had forgotten the thick envelope the Fixer had brought them, in consideration of the service of the Family. He had remembered it, but too late.

The young man was blabbering against Josh's shoulder.

"So I went back inside the Tikki to wrestle it from the damn Thermidor."

"And then?"

"I took it, and pushed the wads in the flour bin. The kitchen was flooding then, but to the roof where Goalie was waiting, calling and calling me.

Josh had seen that bird, owning the roof.

"The wounded one?" he asked.

"That same. Then, I had no choice, as everything was

sinking around me, even the Thermidor is a fish treasure now. I'm not a good swimmer, and less so with that weight. So, I struggled to rip the screen from the back window to pass through, then I climbed to the roof, and waited there..."

Rob stopped there, exhausted. He would need his insulin shot soon.

"Oh, Robbie, you could have died…"

"It's over, big boy, it's over…"

Then there were no more words between them. Rob's slight body filled all the hollows in Josh, the inside hollows, too. He felt a fierce emotion swell inside, something he couldn't deny anymore, pouring from him toward the slender elf he had found in a closet.

Josh did not let go of Rob, indifferent to the rest of the universe. He was conscious of laughs and whoops and whispers around them, of a distant press man reporting on the Safe Harbor pier collapse and "what-do-you-think-mister-mayor", of dozens of blue rectangles of phone screens flipping around like a bunch of hungry gulls, but he didn't care.

ROB WAS COLD, hungry, exhausted, dripping seaweed-smelling water… and happy as a lark. He didn't remember having ridden through such an extreme roller-coaster in his life. He didn't remember feeling so *safe* before, in all the sense of the word.

His arms were wounded around Josh' waist, while his friend's arms was wrapped over his shoulders, the heat radiating through the fabric. Rob had no doubt left, now, that he had found a man worth anything he had thought desirable before. A man who would stand by him, what-ever come.

Who *had* already stood by Rob, at the risk of his own life.

THE TWO MEN eventually detached from each other, a sequence of slow moves, as Josh deposited Rob. They walked toward the Ocean View avenue, entwined, like a dream.

A woman's voice called behind them.

"Hey, you forgot something!"

The pixie girl was running to them in her soaked clothes, her short curls glistening, holding the plastic flour bin in her hands. As she slowed down, Maeve pressed the bin in Josh's arms. Then she turned to get back to her lady friend and the doctor, swift as a swallow.

"Wow," Rob said in a soft voice. "I guess something distracted me."

He tapped the bin's side as they walked away from the crowd, from the smells of popcorn and greasy fries. The event had been a boon for the shops located off the pier. A line had formed near the diner where Rob's sister worked.

THE SUN WAS VERY low now, a distant warmth in their backs as they walked in an amiable silence.

"Hey, big boy, I think you have enough in this pot of gold to open a new place," Rob said, but the tenderness in his tone held another message.

"If you still need a waiter, that is," he added.

Josh could not resist the twinkle in those blue, blue manga eyes.

"Best decision of my life, hiring you," Josh said, one arm wrapped around the bin, the other pressing Rob against him, lifting the younger man's feet off the ground.

They shared a new embrace, with less witnesses this time.

How I love that manga man! Josh thought between kisses. A lone gull flapped over them, calling in this raucous voice. One of its legs was missing.

This time, Josh only heard a benevolent *Haw-haw-haw!*

THE END

ACKNOWLEDGMENTS

The story's inspiration stems from the beauty of the Maine coast, and celebrates the small towns where people cope with environmental and financial difficulties. The town is, of course, entirely fictional.

I read about Thor Heyerdahl's Kon-Tiki expedition as a child. This ocean adventure left me breathless, with the black and white pics of the crew going about, living and cooking on a small surface bobbing on the waves. Hence a shout-out with Josh's Kon Tikki Bar & Restaurant.

At university, I got acquainted with the LGBT community and the tribulations the 'queer' people were going through. One day, a self-righteous believer claimed to me that all gays and lesbians, however good their behavior was, would end up burning in hell. I was so revolted that once I got home, I started writing a poem.

Josh and Rob made their apparition in the first novel of the series, where they get to meet Maeve and Kathleen. I had intertwined part of their back story as a secondary plot line. But then, as the writing of *Safe Harbor* progressed, I felt that Rob and Josh needed their own book for their story to take wing.

Speaking of wings, yes, the one-legged gull is also featured in other stories set in Safe Harbor.

This book is dedicated to my father, Jacques E. Laframboise, who taught me many things, acceptance and patience among them. He has been an humble engineer in love with his work, greeting everyone with an open mind. He encouraged me to pursue my studies in STEM sciences. Even if I did not make a career in that field (I became a science fiction writer instead), he was always celebrating my choices, and he read my manuscripts before everyone else.

Dad was a staunch supporter of justice and social progress. I remember fondly our conversations about the state of the world, while we walked on the road in the Laurentians under a dazzling canopy of stars. For all those hours and the sterling example he set in his life, I am indebted to him.

ABOUT THE AUTHOR

Beside trying to initiate first contact with strange flora, Michèle Laframboise feeds coffee grounds to her garden plants, runs long distances and writes full-time.

Fascinated by sciences and nature since she could walk, she has published 19 novels and over 60 short-stories in French and English, earning various distinctions in Canada and Europe. She is also a comic enthusiast who drew a dozen of graphic novels and maintains an illustrated blog.

Her stories have been featured in Solaris, Galaxies, Fiction River, Compelling Science Fiction, Abyss&Apex, Future SF, Asimov's and Analog. Holding degrees in geography and engineering, she draws from her scientific background to create worlds filled with humor, invention and wonder.

Publisher's website: echofictions.com

Michele's website: michele-laframboise.com

facebook.com/michele.laframboise

twitter.com/savantefolle

instagram.com/michelesff

goodreads.com/sundayartist

ALSO BY MICHÈLE LAFRAMBOISE

Safe Harbor

Climate fiction / friendship / grief / sweet romance

Two torn lives, one generation apart, collide on a polluted
beach. Can two broken women save a dying town?

A witty and heart-warming tale of protecting the place you love,
of finding hope and friendship, told by multi-award winning
author Michèle Laframboise.

ISBN 978-1-988339-94-8 (eBook)

ISBN 978-1-988339-95-5 (paperback)

Condor Cliff

Humor / danger / birdwatching

Trapped in the most beautiful place on Earth, what's a fearless birder to do?

A short and spirited story introducing the energetic and feisty Lady Byrd, written by Michèle Laframboise, multi-award winner SF author and part-time birdwatcher.

ISBN 978-1-988339-02-3 (ePub)

ISBN 978-1-988339-08-5 (paperback)

More books can be found at Echofictions.com

YEARNING FOR MORE?

Michèle Laframboise's full bibliography is enough to whet any SF reader's appetite! Explore it on her official author site at:

michele-laframboise.com

New stories are brewing up constantly!

To get exclusive offers, some free readings, advanced information on special events, join Michele's merry band of readers at :

michele-laframboise.com/fans

FRIENDS' LIST

A story links each reader in a chain of friendship.
Feel free to write your name and give this book to someone close.

_____

_____

_____

_____

_____

_____

_____

_____